THE LEGACY

NECOLE RYSE

Book 1 of The Birthright Trilogy

THE LEGACY

The Legacy
Copyright © 2013 by Necole Ryse
All rights reserved

www.necoleryse.com

ISBN-10: 0692256040
ISBN-13: 978-0692256046

This novel is a work of fiction. Names, characters, places and incidents either are the product of the author's imagination or are used fictitiously. Any resemblance to actual events, locales, organization, or persons living or dead is entirely coincidental and beyond the intent of either the author or the publisher.

Printed in the United States of America

To Ganny – who believed before I did

"It matters not what someone is born,
but what they grow to be."

ALBUS DUMBLEDORE

I needed to get out of the car before I lost every piece of my damn mind. Stuffed in the back seat of my father's Subaru, my legs had been folded under me for only God knew how long during the trek to Ohio. It'd been at least four hours since our last pit stop somewhere in the blur between Pittsburgh and Canton.

My impatient eyes caught my father's weary expression in the rearview mirror. He averted his gaze. I tried to concentrate on something else too, like how my bladder could very well burst any second, or the fact that my mother's hellacious snore could send Helen Keller running.

"We're coming up on the South gate," my father announced. He fidgeted with his tie a bit as we rounded the bin to his alma mater. His knuckles whitened when he gripped the steering wheel. He glanced at his reflection, and then at the road, then back at his reflection again, flicking some invisible speck of nothingness off his goatee.

The whole ride he rambled about how he hadn't been here in over twenty years, and this was the last place he figured he would be right now. I ignored his grumblings, which wasn't hard to do, because my mother's snores practically drowned out any potential conversation we could have had.

Even still, I knew the last thing my father wanted to do was talk to me. He tried the talking method too many times before. All he could do now was take action, which meant packing a bag and driving me cross-country.

I kicked and screamed like any 19-year-old would, but my dad refused to turn around. He and I both knew returning home was not an option. There was nothing waiting there for me but a district attorney who, if he could, would throw me under the jail.

And of course there was Antoine.

I tried to push the memory of his last kiss out of my mind. Sometimes, I still tasted the blood that pooled in my mouth that day or the way his hands quivered when he held me.

I shook the memory away as we made a sharp turn onto Fitzgerald Avenue.

Our car trembled back and forth as we drove over the cobblestone. Our tires slipped, losing traction in the snow. We passed under a rusted metal sign that either welcomed our arrival or my death. Intricate cast iron gates stretched toward the dreary sky and dozens of expensive cars lined the narrow suburban street.

Then, seemingly out of nowhere, a slew of brick buildings emerged, only one standing out from the others. Its roof, brushed with a metallic gold, caught the sunrays effortlessly and showered the snow-covered lawn. Bits of snow sparkled like lightning bugs after dark.

"This is Benjamin Fitz." My dad slowed to a stop.

Now I see why he wore that ridiculous tie.

"You went to school *here?*" My eyes scanned over the matching buildings. Everything looked so perfect, so rich, so not like me...so not like us. I tugged on the collar of my too big sweatshirt. This was going to be a disaster.

"Is that so surprising?" He scoffed, pulling his good sports coat from the hanger that swayed back and forth in my peripheral in the seven-hour ride from Maryland. He only wore it on Easter morning services and funerals.

This was obviously my funeral.

"I wasn't expecting this," I said to myself, which just so happened to be out loud. I honestly didn't know what to expect, but it wasn't this.

"Consider yourself lucky." He cut his eyes at me. "This wasn't easy."

My father pulled some strings, well a lot of strings if you let him tell it, at his alma mater. See, Benjamin Wallace Fitzgerald was supposed to be some fancy-smancy Ivy League school for African Americans. Most high school or transfer students couldn't even apply if their parents or grandparents didn't attend. The students with lineage at the school were called Legacies. Non-Legacies, as my dad told me, almost never get in. The non-legacies that do, though, were supposedly Einstein smart on a coveted scholarship.

It made me wonder. If my father were a legacy of this supposed prestigious institution, how'd he end up working construction in Maryland? Or driving a 1997 Subaru that most likely wouldn't make the trek back home? How did we end up going to bed with growling stomachs if this place promised such a wonderful future?

Once again, my eyes found his. He read my inquisitive expression. We didn't speak but I knew his thoughts.

"Let's get you inside." He wrapped a knit scarf around his neck and ventured into the brutal cold.

An icy wind whipped through the car when the driver's side door opened and slammed shut, startling my mother from her four-hour hibernation. I caught her ghostly reflection in the side mirror.

"Oh, Rae," she gushed, pushing herself up in the seat. Her stringy hair stuck in place like a rooster's crown. "This was more than I imagined," she said breathlessly, taking in the scenery around her. She slipped her fragile frame into her bulky winter coat. "It's so beautiful."

I had to admit this place was most definitely the makings of a fairytale, but I certainly wasn't the kind of girl who had fairytale endings. I had a boyfriend, but he was certainly no prince charming on a white horse. More like a convicted felon in a 1977 souped up Crown Victoria.

Don't ask.

Just ahead, a body came into view, running up the walkway toward us.

"Um, Dad?" I called. "I think our welcoming committee has arrived."

"Well, aren't you going to get out?" I knew it wasn't a question. Tingles spread all over when I unfolded my legs. I shrugged on my coat and zipped it up to my neck.

My mother began to zip her coat too when my dad called to her, "Just Raevyn, honey. Uh, stay inside, it's too cold. We won't be long." She snapped her seatbelt back into place without another word.

I glanced back at my father who nudged me with his eyes. I stayed put as the stranger neared. His tan trench coat, knotted at his slim waist, forced my eyes to travel to his broad, athletic shoulders. A thick olive scarf hid most of his face. His dark washed denim clung to his thighs and were tucked neatly into a pair of impeccable Polo Conquest boots. He bounced on his toes when he walked, you know, how most rich people do when they don't have a care in the world. His whole demeanor read that he was born and bred right in the lap of luxury of Fitzgerald County. I could smell his spoiled brat attitude from a mile away.

And it stunk.

I hopped out of the car and the salted cobblestone crunched under my worn Timberland boots. The cold seeped in sometimes, stabbing my toes, where the suede was separating from the sole.

"Rae," my dad said through his plastered smile. "You introduce yourself with your full name to every person you meet here," he finished just as Mr. Welcoming Committee slowed to a stop a few footsteps away.

"Raevyn Elizabeth Jones," Welcoming Committee boomed. He pulled his scarf down around his neck, exposing his full lips that sat beneath a perfectly groomed mustache. His breathtaking brown eyes, so mysteriously dark, almost as if they were black, smiled at me behind oversized nerd glasses.

"That's me." I folded my arms over my chest. I glanced over at my father, and he turned his lips up at me disapprovingly. Should I have curtsied or something? I extended my hand and Welcoming Committee stripped off his matching olive leather glove. His warm hand wrapped firmly, magnetically around mine.

"Pleasure to meet you."

I snatched my hand away, burying it safely inside my jacket pocket. His touch lingered there.

"Charles Alexander Jones." My father cut in. "You're a little young to be the Dean of Students. I thought Dr. Rudd would meet us here this morning."

"Forgive me," he started. "I'm merely Dr. Rudd's assistant. He's unfortunately sick this morning, but he wanted someone to meet you at the gate when you arrived."

"I'm sorry to hear that." My father blew out a breath. It was hard to tell whether he was relieved or disappointed.

"I'm Jeffrey Vincent Eugene Donnelly the fourth, and I'll be walking you to your dorm."

"To the door, correct?" My father jumped in again. "You ain't walking my daughter inside."

"Of course not, sir. Each dormitory has a housemother or father, respectively. She will have your room assignment and your schedule of classes, things of that nature," he backtracked. My father was a big guy. He had every right to be nervous.

I snorted a laugh.

"Give us a minute," my dad said to Jeffrey, who gladly retreated. I guessed he caught on pretty quickly that my dad meant business. Usually, when he said something, you did it and there would be no further discussion. According to my dad, that was my problem lately. I felt the need to discuss everything. He dragged me to the back of the Subaru, out of Jeffrey's earshot.

"Now when you get in here you need to act like you have some sense," he warned, wagging his finger at me.

"Why do I have to impress these people?"

"Do you know how many people I had to call? How much begging I had to do to get your application seen?"

I rolled my eyes while he slammed my suitcase to the ground. He didn't seem to understand that he didn't have to do any of this. I was perfectly fine with the life that I lived in Maryland.

Real college was never in the cards for me, anyway. I did a few semesters at MCC to appease my dad, but Antoine and I were supposed to move away and start a new life together. Of course all of that got ruined in the summer, but that only gave us more ammunition. I just needed more time to change the plan. He and I would be together one way or another. It didn't matter how many miles my dad tried to put between us. My father kept calling the accident a blessing. He kept saying the accident was a chance to turn my life around. Oh, please. That accident was a nightmare. It was the worst thing that happened to my relationship. Now, I realized that Benjamin Wallace Fitzgerald was the worst thing that happened to my relationship.

I've seen my dad staring at his degree that he kept in the kitchen's junk drawer. This was the life *he* left behind. It wasn't right for him to force it on me. He could keep his stupid traditions and curtsies and ball gowns. It hasn't gotten him anywhere. Why would this place be any different for me?

"What am I supposed to say to these people? We don't have anything in common. Dad, look at his clothes!" I jerked my head in Jeffrey's direction.

"You introduce yourself, every time, with your full name."

I sighed, waving him away, but he continued, "If they ask your legacy, and they will," he stressed, "you tell them your lineage. Reginald Wilfred Jones of the Jones Funeral Home in Atlanta."

"Atlanta? I've never even been to Atlanta!" I stomped my foot, which landed in a mound of snow. *Great, just great*, I thought.

"Just say it, Raevyn! How hard is it to follow directions? You'll probably live in the freshman dorms. Those are just ahead of the Fitz statue in the courtyard. Are you listening? You have to blend in here!"

"This is for your own good," my mother chimed in from the front seat.

"Blend in? This is ridiculous." I kicked the snow from my boot against the bumper of the car. How the hell was I supposed to blend with these people? We had nothing in common but the color of our skin. I might as well be a damn space alien. "I guess I don't have a choice."

"No, you don't." He lifted my chin towards his face. "Just keep your nose clean, keep your head down, and behave, Raevyn."

I pushed him away. "You act like I'm going to burn the place down." I grabbed the broken handle of my rickety second-hand suitcase and stomped to the front of the car. I heard the familiar sputtering of the engine. My mother gave a sorrowful wave from the front seat.

"Don't joke like that." My dad followed closely behind. He wrapped his arms around my lifeless body. "Try to make the best of it, Rae…" His voice cracked. "Because you know you can't come home."

"You take care of my baby," he threatened Jeffrey.

"Yes, sir." Jeffrey nodded, taking my suitcase. He stood patiently, waiting for the goodbyes to end.

"Rae?" my dad called to me again, just before our silence became awkward. I turned back to him, and he mouthed, "I love you."

I wanted to say something back. I wanted to scream so many things to him. But there was nothing I could say that I hadn't already said. I told him it was unfair. I made it clear that I wanted nothing to do with college. I kicked. I screamed. I scratched. I punched. But he still brought me here. And now my life was over.

"I'm ready, Jeffrey," I lied.

I took a deep breath. The cold air pierced my throat. I couldn't face the sight of my parents backing down the driveway, leaving me here, almost five hundred miles away from everything I'd ever known.

"Let's go," Jeffrey said, before the thought to hop right back in the car with my parents bloomed in my mind.

"You only have this one bag?" Jeffrey readjusted his hand around the broken handle. One side was snapped off, making the bag hard to navigate. Finally, he gave up, and tucked it under his arm. The tall, black iron gates squeaked closed behind us, locking us in. The Subaru's daytime lights swept the driveway and pulled onto the main road. The engine's familiar sputter faded away.

They left.

They really left me here.

I threw my shoulders back and pulled my faux leather coat tightly around me. I dipped my chin into my scarf and nodded in Jeffrey's direction.

"Yeah, just this." I followed his lead away from the South gate and into the brick-lined campus. Majestic in its own right and breathtakingly spotless, but all I could see was a prison. I guessed Antoine and I were one in the same. "Why? You want to carry my purse too?"

"I've never seen anything like this." He looked down at me through his lenses. "You're low maintenance."

I spent all of five minutes with him and he already commented on my lack of stuff. Rich kids were so spoiled. I bet all of the students at Fitz were like this; taking inventory of each others possessions, weighing their value on the weight of their suitcase. There was no way in hell I could blend in here.

"Most Atlanta girls come with five and six bags and that's just for their shoes."

I rolled my eyes at his attempts at small talk. It was too damn cold for small talk.

"I'm from Maryland." The words jumped out of my mouth before I could stop them. *Shit!* I thought. I was supposed to be from Atlanta. I talked through my mishap. "I figure I'll be home in a few weeks for Christmas break. I didn't need a bunch of things," I snapped, unable to take the edge out of my voice.

"I'm sure," he said. "Except you probably won't go home for break. You've missed a lot of school. There's no way you can catch up in a few weeks. You'll stay through the break more than likely." He hooked a right at the end of the sidewalk.

"Stay…here?"

"It isn't that bad. Lots of people stay through breaks. We're open all year thanks to him."

Just then, we rounded a life-sized statue of some old guy in the middle of a snow-covered courtyard. I figured this was the infamous Benjamin Wallace Fitzgerald. He was standing with his arms stretched outwards as if he were in the midst of a lecture. Wire glasses skimmed the bridge of his wide nose. I slowed my pace. My eyes caught a glimpse of a metal plate. The words BLACK EXCELLENCE were carved there. Below it, in smaller print was the phrase, 'Ivy league education for us—for all.'

Jeffrey stole a look at his watch. "Breakfast begins at eight a.m. There's morning service and announcements at nine a.m., then the day will begin, business as usual. It's almost seven so I'll give you some time to settle in. After announcements, though, you'll be on your own."

I automatically headed towards the freshman dormitories just ahead of the Fitz statue like my dad said when I realized Jeffrey wasn't beside me anymore.

"Where are you going?" he and I both said at the same time.

"You're this way." He beckoned over his shoulder.

"Freshman dorms are this way," I countered.

"Low maintenance and knowledgeable." Jeffrey counted on his invisible tally. "Except you're in the sophomore honors dormitory. From the looks of your application, you're more than qualified for this school."

Honors? This must have been a mistake. "Wait, you've seen my application?" If he saw my application then he knew I was poor, not low maintenance. If he saw my application, would he know who I really was?

"No," he admitted, "but you've got to be very accomplished to have Dr. Rudd call me at five a.m. to personally escort you to your dorm."

"This," I stammered, "this doesn't happen to everybody?"

I ran ahead, catching up with him.

"Most parents don't even bother showing up. I've never seen anything like it." The balls of his cheeks skimmed his glasses. I ripped my eyes from his and concentrated on the ground. I concentrated on my damp sock. I concentrated on Antoine, my boyfriend. But, I couldn't help wondering if his parents showed up on his first day. The only sound between us now was the constant crunch of salt and ice beneath our feet.

Before long, we were at the steps of the Gwendolyn Boyd Honors Dormitory.

"All right, Miss Ambitious." Jeffrey handed over my tattered suitcase like it was a baby. "Up the stairs and right inside you'll find Mrs. Potts. She'll show you to your room."

"Thanks for walking me." Was I supposed to curtsy now?

"Low-maintenance, knowledgeable *and* thankful," he said. "Your list of qualities keeps growing and growing. The pleasure was all mine Raevyn Elizabeth Jones. I'll see you around," he said before taking off.

I watched as he rounded the corner by the William Fitz statue. While he walked away, I wondered how many of these rich girls fell for his game.

I traveled up the steps and stopped at the door of the Boyd dormitory. The worn doorknob, which was once a vibrant gold, had been turned so much that the paint had long since faded away. Because of its shabbiness, the knob turned with ease. Immediately, heat fought the frigid air forcing entry. The scent of citrus and cinnamon engulfed me once the door slammed.

Surprisingly, it felt like home.

An enormous floral arrangement of poinsettias in the foyer blocked my view of the living room. Strategically placed garland ran along the walls, sure not to cover the black and white framed photographs of women, which, I assumed, lived here during their time at Benjamin W. Fitzgerald.

An oversized Christmas tree leaned in a far corner. Too tall for the room, the tip sagged sadly against the ceiling. Burgundy and gold gaudy ornaments hung off the edges. Small artificial doves floated playfully in and out of the branches while multi-colored string lights blinked at an odd pace. This was definitely the work of someone's grandmother.

When I reached the foyer, a little elderly woman stood, waiting for me—the decorator. Her head was a lumpy mess full of rollers tied in a silk scarf. Dark freckles spotted her thin nose and diamonds, the size of dimes, glistened in her ears. She clutched a cup of steaming liquid and when her small, watery eyes met mine her smile took over her face.

"You must be Raevyn."

"Yes ma'am," I answered, extending my hand. "Raevyn Elizabeth Jones."

"Lovely." She approved. "That's all you got?" She pointed to my bag.

"Yes ma'am, I thought I would only be here for a few weeks." We walked through the foyer toward a narrow hallway. A fluorescent red sign glowed threateningly at the end, its buzz echoing annoyingly loud.

"What's that?"

"Emergency exit," she answered without looking. "If you push it open, the alarm sounds. It's a whole big mess. The administration upped the security 'round here last year so now you need a swipe card to get in and out of the emergency exits." She pat her pocket. "I have the only one for this building."

A cramped elevator opened automatically at our presence and we boarded. She pressed button 3 and it churned to a start.

"Anyway," she continued, "I will send a car to retrieve your other bags."

A car? "That's not necessary. I'll make do with this."

"It's no problem," she insisted. "We can send someone as early as this afternoon. You must only have a couple of outfits in there. That's not nearly enough for all the time you'll be here." The doors clambered open and we both stepped off the elevator. She made a sharp right down a long hallway of French style doors. Thick carpet ran the length of the hardwood floor and millions of women in framed pictures followed me with their eyes.

"But, I live in Maryland," I said. "That would take forever."
Atlanta! I repeated in my head. *You live in Atlanta!*

"You don't have to worry about that," she said, totally ignoring my refusal. "Someone will pick up your clothes, and then you'll have everything you need."

"This…" I swallowed slowly, debating with myself. If I didn't tell her she'd keep asking and insisting. She'd keep talking and pressing me. "…this is all I have."

She stopped in her tracks so quickly that I almost ran into the back of her. Her body turned slowly as she faced me. She studied me like a textbook. "Jones, is it?" she inquired.

"Yes ma'am," I answered her, feeling heat creep up my neck.

"You wouldn't happen to be related to Reginald Wilfred Jones of the Jones Funeral Home in Atlanta?"

I nodded slowly, swallowing the rock in my throat. I was doing a terrible job of blending.

"And *that's* all you have?" she asked again, pointing to my bag.

I nodded, burning all over now, and before I knew it, she pulled me in for a tight embrace. Her head stopped at my chest. The ends of her rollers stabbed through my jacket. "We'll take good care of you." She released me and turned toward the door.

"This is your room." She cleared her throat and began another conversation like nothing had happened. She dug into her pocket and retrieved a long golden key. I'd only seen one like that in movies. She pressed it into my palm and my fingers curled around it.

"We only have one other key like this, so don't lose it," she said. "Your class schedule is loaded on your laptop inside and oh"—she handed me the steaming cup—"this is yours."

"Thank you very much," I whispered, filing that awkward hug moment away in my mind.

"I'm on the first floor, room 100. It's right off the foyer if you ever need anything," she said. "You can get some rest for a few minutes, but breakfast starts right at eight. I assure you, get there early. Try the omelettes by Gary."

"Do I have a roommate?" I asked just as she started to scurry down the hallway.

"Regina Larisse Fitzgerald," she answered over her shoulder before getting back on the elevator. I heard the doors open then close and it began its labored descend.

Once I was inside, my jaw dropped so hard I thought it was dislocated. There was no way this was my life. Years ago, when Antoine and I started to date, he took me to a hotel in D.C. We shared a beautiful suite, and until today, was the largest room I'd ever stayed in.

I placed my hot chocolate on the nearest ledge and dropped my bag. I slipped my boots off, careful not to tread any salt through the room. Beside me, a fifty, maybe sixty-inch flat screen television hung off the wall. A low flame smoldered in the electric fireplace below. The mantle was decorated with random knick-knacks, trophies, and professional pictures all signed in loopy handwriting by a beautiful smiling girl, Regina L. Fitz.

I pulled the picture off the mantle, hoping my eyes were playing tricks on me, and my heart dropped through my stomach. My roommate was a *Fitzgerald?* It was just my luck that my roommate would be a great-great-great-granddaughter of the founder of this school. The entire car ride over I prayed that I wouldn't get paired with a posh, too-cute-for-you, princess chick, and judging from the miniature Eifel towers and French poodles that danced along the mantle—not to mention the dozens of accolades—I was sure God forwarded those prayers to his voicemail. I carefully replaced the picture and stumbled into the arm of the L-shaped sectional that stretched the length of the room. A towering bookshelf stood beyond the couch, its shelves spilling over with books. To the left was a small table, I assumed for eating and studying, and beyond that was an enormous bay window. I ran over and pulled the blinds open, looking down at the sidewalk in front of the dormitory. Light flooded in, striking the bronze crown molding that ran around the perimeter of the room. Despite my potential roommate troubles, I could get used to living inside an Ikea catalog.

"Great string pulling, Dad."

Another pair of French doors were at both ends of the room. One door had a pop of pink ribbon tied around the handle, dangling a paper R, obviously for Regina. I headed to the other set of doors with the naked knobs and pushed it open.

I paid no attention to the beautiful furniture or the perfect decor. My eyes zeroed in on one thing. On top of the desk, at the foot of the bed was, just as Mrs. Potts said, a brand new laptop.

I picked it up and looked around a few times, hoping it wasn't one of those fake cardboard ones at department stores that were used for decoration. But, it wasn't. It was new and it was mine. I pressed the power button and the laptop sang its welcome. The screen automatically opened up to my class schedule:

Benjamin Wallace Fitzgerald 2013-2014

Raevyn E. Jones

Student #0505917

M/W/F: African American History – 10 AM

Advanced Calculus – 2 PM

Intro to French – 5 PM.

T/Th: Mass Comm. 215 – 11 AM

Political Science 2 – 3 PM

Advanced *what?* I looked at the schedule over and over hoping it would change. It didn't.

"Too many strings, Dad," I mumbled.

A window popped out of nowhere. An instant message covered the whole screen.

Good morning, Raevyn E. Jones. I am your academic advisor for the 2013-2014 school year here at the prestigious Benjamin Wallace Fitzgerald University. Please meet me in my office, Student Services building, room 305, as soon as you receive this message.

S. Tanner

I pulled my jacket back on and slipped my feet into my boots that were left by the door. I downed a few gulps of hot chocolate and stuffed the long key in my purse.

It didn't occur to me until I was outside, and shielding my face from the whipping wind, that I had no idea where I was going. For just a second I wished Jeffrey could guide me again. I figured I would head in the opposite direction of the South gate at the back of campus.

I walked briskly past the Fitz statue. It seemed like his eyes were following me, judging me, asking me what the hell my Payless shoes were doing walking on his brick lined campus. I studied each matchy-matchy modern building until I noticed one standing catty corner at the end of a walkway. The pillar beside it read: Student Services.

I hurried inside wanting more than anything to feel heat circulate through my bones again. I shook the bit of snow out of my hair. The saturated locks slapped against my face. I pulled it into a messy braid that fell over my shoulder.

Room 305 was not hard to find because my academic advisor, Miss Tanner, was the only person in the deserted building. Her voice echoed against the eggshell washed walls.

I wasn't greeted when I walked in. A scary woman, probably near the brink of malnutrition, judging from the way her skin hung off her bones, gestured to an empty seat on the other side of her wooden desk that seemed to swallow her skeletal frame whole. A thick pair of bifocals sat on the end of her long, skinny nose, and her dark beady eyes sunk deep into her brown face.

Her desk didn't hold much, not even a spec of dust. Every pen sat upright, as if by magical force, together in a black coffee mug that read FITZ ALUM, with their logos facing outwards. She had a small Blackberry glued to her ear and gave me the 'hold on' finger when I sat down.

I hated the rich; always holding up someone else's time but demanding that theirs was not wasted.

"You'll just have to flunk her, Randy. She knows the rules. If she misses more than four classes unexcused then she will have to retake the class."

She listened for a bit to the guy on the other end, rolling her eyes at whatever he was saying. She examined her cuticles for a second and then turned her attention to me, the only thing in her office that hadn't been wiped down and sanitized. Her cold eyes slid over my hair and face, then down to my coat and graffiti jeans. If she could, I'm sure she would have slouched down in her seat to see what kind of shoes I wore. So discreet, the rich.

I made sure to keep eye contact to let her know I was watching her watch me. She gave me a forced grin, one that is learned from years of being phony. I made sure not to return it.

"I understand," she said, getting right back to business. She pulled an emery board out of her desk and began to scratch away at the only healthy looking thing on her body—her nails. "But rules are rules. I will talk to Headmaster today but I'm sure she's missed too much of the semester to continue. She has to come back next fall. Besides, her replacement is here already." She paused for a second and spoke loudly over Randy. "If Mrs. Wheeler has a problem with it, tell her she can call me. She's spent way too much time in that psych ward if she thinks her kid can waltz back into my pre-honors program with a 2.8 GPA." She scoffed. "I mean, really. Who did she think she was fooling?"

I heard Randy cackle through the speaker. "I gotta go. I'll call you at lunch." She sat the phone down and finished shaping her pinky nail.

She replaced the emery board and said, "Now onto you." She huffed as if I intruded on her personal time, and pulled a thick file out of her desk. It landed with a thump, making the pens in her cup tremble. "Raevyn Elizabeth Jones." She adjusted her glasses. "Hmm, pre-honors program," she mumbled, flipping a few pages. Her eyes locked onto mine.

"You do know that the pre-honors program here at B. W. Fitz is competitive? You must keep a 3.5 GPA at all times. I see here you've only had one year of community college education."

She flipped a few more photocopied pages and I noticed my transcript from my community college.

She chuckled. "Oh, this can't be right." She reached for her phone to dial someone when she looked over at me as if she forgot I was in the room already.

Her eyes scanned the page. "You haven't taken any Advanced Placement classes in high school." She flipped through a handful of pages and said, "Why, you've barely squeaked by your whole life." How far did that thing go back?

"The pre-honors program is no place for someone like you. Maybe your father can try some place easier like say, A&T or Clark-Atlanta? Has Morris Brown finally closed? I know a few people in admissions—"

"Excuse me?" I bristled.

Her ears perked at my attitude and she readjusted herself in her seat. Little Miss Malnutrition was ready for war.

"Benjamin Wallace Fitzgerald is not a cake walk, Miss Jones. From the looks of things you would barely qualify for the comprehensive program. I'll talk to Dr. Rudd when he gets in because these classes are way too advanced for someone with your level of education."

My heartbeat quickened. Blood revved, preparing to shoot through my veins. I buried my hands under my legs, preventing my fingers from curling into a fist. "My classes are fine."

"Oh, of course." She fiddled with the thin string of pearls around her neck. "It's not the classes I'm worried about, honey. This school is about prestige and honor. There are kids who are dying to receive an education of such standard. I don't know how Dr. Rudd got you in, or who he *thinks* you are, but he can't expect me to let you waltz in here with these below average scores and boot one of my deserving kids out for you."

"That sounds like a personal problem. I got in. I'll maintain your bullshit GPA and I'll be fine."

Her mouth flattened into a straight line. "You slip one point below a 3.5 young lady and I'll make sure to have you on the first thing smoking back to your little community college. Where you belong."

I stood up so quick her precious cup of pens toppled over, scattering across her desk like roaches in light. Her breath caught in her throat. She probably thought I would punch her teeth in. But, I realized it wouldn't be a fair fight. She looked like she weighed ninety pounds soaking wet. In one punch, with my weak hand, she'd be in a coma. And I'd be back in Maryland, without that laptop. She wasn't worth it.

"Are we done?" I pulled my purse back onto my shoulder.

She nodded, swallowing the lump of fear that was lodged in her throat. I swatted at a picture frame that sat on the edge of her desk for good measure. It teetered a bit before crashing to the ground.

"I'll be keeping a close eye on you," she called after me.

I pushed open the door and trekked back to my dorm.

In my first hour at Benjamin Wallace Fitzgerald University I already had an enemy. My dad would not be pleased.

The whole walk back to my dorm I struggled between laughing and berating myself for letting Miss Tanner get under my skin. I knew I had to keep a low profile, but if anyone else here was anything like my advisor, I'd beat my father back to Maryland.

My room was exactly the same as I left it. My schedule was still up on my computer screen and, although intimidating, I wasn't going to let Miss Tanner win. I had to blend.

To the right of the desk was a sliding door that led to a huge walk-in closet, the size of my bedroom in Maryland. I didn't own enough clothes to cover a quarter of the racks. Staring at the bare racks reminded me that in a little less than an hour, I was supposed to be at breakfast with the rest of the students. I grimaced at my jeans and mismatched socks. I thought about Jeffrey in his expensive trench coat and designer jeans. How was I supposed to blend with clothes like these?

I rummaged through my suitcase, turning over pairs of over worn jeans and faded cartoon T-shirts. I had a few sweaters. Only one was a name brand, a purple Lacoste sweater Antoine bought for me a few Christmases ago when we took matching photos. It was probably about four or five seasons old, but it was the best thing I could find to blend into the slew of rich kids.

I kicked the suitcase deep into the closet and slammed it shut. I walked toward my four-piece bathroom on the other side of my desk. My mirror image stared back at me above a marble sink. I ran my fingers over the weft of the braid that cascaded over my shoulder. My large almond eyes were burning red from lack of sleep on the drive. My cheeks and nose were flushed from the harsh winter cold. I looked like a fish out of water. Like I didn't belong.

I switched out of my clothes hastily and undid my braid, letting my hair fall over my shoulders. The time it had been in the braid curled my hair in a beautiful wave pattern that reached the middle of my back.

I fiddled around with my hair when I noticed a shadow pass through the constant stream of natural light. My breathing slowed when I heard a set of muffled footsteps creep closer and as soon as I whipped around a white flash blinded me. A searing pain zipped up my arm when a set of long nails dug into my skin.

"Caught you!" someone screamed. "I knew you were up here sneaking around in Brooke's room. It was only a matter of time."

My first instinct was to swing, hoping my fist collided with something. I rubbed the white dots out of my eyes. "I'm Raevyn Jones."

Shit, whole name!

"It doesn't matter who you are," she spat, dragging me away. My feet stumbled over each other. "I'm taking you to Mrs. Potts. I kept telling her the janitors were up here in Brooke's room."

"Janitor?" I belted out. "I'm not the janitor!"

"Oh yeah? Then why are you dressed like that?"

I was dressed like a *janitor*? I gripped the edge of the doorframe, planted my feet and pulled away from her. She fumbled for my arm again. I drew back and dared her to touch me again.

"I am Raevyn Elizabeth Jones. This is my room," I said as calm as possible, feeling the heat rise to my cheeks. If we were in Maryland, this girl would not be standing.

"You're Brooke's replacement? You're...the new girl?"

I nodded as my normal vision slowly swam into place. A wave of embarrassing realization washed over the tall, brown skinned girl in front of me. A humiliating smile crept onto her face. Her Scooby-Doo pajama pants were too short, cutting off way above the respectable point for highwaters. Her shirt ended right before her belly button. I eyed a sparkle from a ring hanging from her navel. She crossed her arms over her chest and chewed her French tipped nail.

"I'm so sorry." She breathed, touching the same arm she grabbed a few seconds ago. I ripped it away. Her dark hair, curled in flexi-rods, stuck all over her head like snakes. Her perfectly arched eyebrows rose in apology while she said, "I'm Regina Larisse Fitzgerald of Benjamin Wallace Fitzgerald University. And your roommate." She tried to smile sweetly, as if she hadn't already accused me of being the help.

"Raevyn Elizabeth Jones."

"Of course," she gushed. "Raevyn Jones of...?"

Say the legacy, Raevyn. "The Jones Funeral Home in Atlanta."

"No wonder why you're dressed like that." She turned, sashaying back inside of our room. "All of you southerners dress weird."

I followed her, fiddling with the hem of my sweater. I had to remember that everyone here was a legacy. Everyone here came from a lineage of wealth. If I wanted to fly under the radar, I had to keep up with the Jones'. No pun intended.

"Were you heading out for breakfast?" she asked over her shoulder.

"Yeah," I heard myself say. "Mrs. Potts said to get there early."

"Just wait a sec. My friend usually comes over and we go together. I would love for you to meet the crew." She smiled and beckoned me to her room.

Here's one thing I learned about Regina Larisse Fitzgerald only from walking about three steps into her room: she had obsessive-compulsive disorder big time. She didn't do rituals and tap her pointer finger against the doorknob eight times when she woke up, no, that's not it. What I saw was much worse than that.

Regina was a neat freak.

Nothing in her room was out of place. I expected maybe a few papers strewn about, maybe a laptop open and a pair of jeans draped over the edge of the bed. There was nothing of the sort. I felt like I was trapped inside of a *Martha Stewart Living* magazine. 'Ooh la la' was decaled above her bed in a curvy font that stretched the length of the wall.

The heavy scent of Chanel No.5 hung in the air, confrontational and aggressive. Antoine stole a whole box of it off a Macy's truck one Christmas and the bottles shattered in his trunk. Needless to say, his entire car smelled like the stuff for about a year and a half. I'd know the scent anywhere.

"You can have a seat." She gestured to her perfectly made canopy bed. "Mind the pillows, please."

I lowered myself on the comforter, making sure not to wrinkle it. She would probably steam clean it or something when I left.

I watched her cross the room to her closet, which was also decaled, go figure, with an Eifel tower split right down the middle where the double doors met. When she swung the doors open, I couldn't stop my mouth from dropping open. There were no empty spaces on her racks like mine. I couldn't even see a rack to be quite honest. Shelves lined the back walls with shoes from bejeweled flats to strappy high heels and platform pumps to knee-high boots and athletic tennis shoes. All of her clothes were color coordinated from winter white to the deepest blacks and every single color you could imagine in between.

"You know," she began, leaning her shoulder on the frame. "I really wish I had a casual knee-length dress. I just need something simple today." She tapped her acrylic nail against her teeth making an annoying clicking sound.

"You're telling me you don't have that in there?" I scoffed, salivating on the edge of her bed. I was sure if I got any closer to her closet I'd drool all over myself.

"Not necessarily," she said, walking inside. The closet swallowed her. "I wish I could see everything at once," she said, "I mean, this thing is half the size of my one at home. It's ridiculous they can't give us bigger closets." She had *more* clothes?

"Where are you from?" I asked, probably sounding annoyed that her regular closet was bigger than my entire kitchen. Some girls have it all.

"Chicago." She pulled a black bodycon dress off the hanger and slipped it over her head. It stopped short just above her knees. If she breathed hard she would burst out of the thing.

"What do you think?" She looked over at me probably waiting for me to give her amazing fashion advice. Instead, I wanted to tell her to take the thing off.

I opened my mouth knowing that what would come out wouldn't be supportive. I thought we were just going to breakfast. Was there a nightclub between here and the cafeteria?

"You need a blazer," another voice interjected before I could respond. "Isn't that the backless Calvin Klein?"

Backless? A dark skinned girl with high cheekbones and red, full lips sashayed into the room and flopped on the bed. Her enormous designer bag clunked against the floor. She pulled her ear buds out and the bouncy beat floated in the air.

"Yeah, but it's casual, right? Blazer and these boots," Regina asked, bringing a pair of dark brown knee-high boots to her leg.

That's *casual?*

"Perfect," the stranger acknowledged, without looking over.

The room grew silent. *Should I introduce myself?* She glanced over at me, looking me up and down as if she just recognized there was someone else in the room.

"Regina, you getting your closet door fixed again?" Her features were striking, like she was handmade by a meticulous manufacturer and plucked out of a Barbie advertisement.

"No, why?" Regina answered, pulling the flexi rods from her hair at her vanity.

"Then…what's *she* doing here?"

Regina slapped her hand over her mouth. I wanted to respond and tell her exactly what I was doing here. Instead, I bit down hard on the inside of my cheek, distracting myself with pain.

"This is the new girl—Brooke's replacement. She's from Atlanta, right?" Regina asked for confirmation, looking at me in the mirror, like being from Atlanta explained everything.

"Raevyn Elizabeth Jones," I reported, neglecting to extend my hand.

"Oh, sorry." She popped up. "Andrea Renee Terrell of the Terrell Music Group in Washington, D.C." She hadn't stopped looking me up and down while she introduced herself and it was getting annoying.

"What are you looking at?" I snapped. Well, there goes my attempt to blend.

She didn't flinch. "You going natural or something?"

"Andreaaaaa," Regina whined, running a paddle brush through her curls. "Would you quit?"

"Just a question." She shrugged, popping one ear bud back into her ear. Her black B. W. Fitz blazer was closed tightly across her enormous chest. A camel colored belt cinched her waist and she too wore a black dress with knee-high boots. If this was the uniform, no wonder why I stuck out like a sore thumb. No wonder the both of them thought I fixed light bulbs for a living.

"No, but seriously, are you?" she asked, flicking her unbelievably long fake hair over her shoulder.

"My hair is just naturally curly," I answered with attitude.

"That's not a weave?" the both of them asked simultaneously.

"Shit, girl, I thought that was a weave." Andrea laughed uneasily. "You gon' comb it or something?"

"Do I look *that* bad?"

Both of them shot each other uneasy looks before answering.

"Oh, don't get shy now."

"Girl, take that damn sweater off." Andrea demanded. She stood up, and her height literally dwarfed both Regina and I.

"Drea's a model," Regina said, like she could read my mind. "She's modeled overseas for a bit before coming to Fitz. She's like 30 years old."

I felt my eyes pop. "She's lying," Andrea countered. "I'm only twenty. But being one year older than these girls, and being well traveled, makes me feel like the eldest out of the bunch."

"The bunch?" I asked as Andrea gestured for me to stand up. She walked over, picking at my sweater before finally lifting it over my head. She struggled getting it over my big hair.

"Yeah, it's a couple of us," Regina chimed in. "You'll meet everyone at breakfast." She pulled her eyelid down to apply a thick coat of liner.

"What are you like a size ten? Twelve?" Andrea asked, feeling my waist. She bit down on her bottom lip, tracing circles around me.

"Something like that," I answered, neglecting the urge to slap her hands away. "Sometimes, I can squeeze into an eight."

Regina and her exchanged quick glances. What was it with them? "What are you guys like size two's?" I stole a long glance at Andrea while she fiddled in Regina's closet.

"Six, honey." Andrea whipped her weave over her shoulder.

"Same," Regina answered, applying probably the third coat of a pale pink gloss.

"Tell me you have something she can wear from your fat days," Andrea called, moving toward the back of Regina's closet.

"Fat days?" I exclaimed.

"You'll have to forgive Andrea," Regina cut in. "She doesn't have any manners."

Oh, really? I couldn't tell.

"Take it or leave it." Andrea shrugged, moving hangers around. She pulled a dress off the rack, stared at it and then back at me. Her nose wrinkled in disgust. She eyed a dark purple dress then looked over at me, opportunity dancing in her eyes.

"No." I backed up. "I'd look like Barney in that."

"Child, please. You looked like Barney in that damn sweater. How old is that thing anyway?"

"My boyfriend got it for me a couple years back." I felt a pang in my heart at the thought of Antoine again. We'd never been so far apart before.

"Oh, please tell me he's your ex." She looked up at me before helping me out of my jeans and shoes. "Boyfriends buy diamonds, honey. Remember that."

How could I tell these girls that my boyfriend wasn't actually my ex and I prided myself on that sweater? How could I tell them that my boyfriend was actually a convicted felon awaiting trial in jail right now? They would probably run screaming if I told them the truth. I couldn't tell them. I wouldn't tell them.

"Of course." I forced a laugh, fidgeting with the zipper on the dress. "Can't bring sand to the beach." I stepped in the garment and Andrea promptly zipped it.

"Oh, you're my kind of girl," Regina said, turning toward her vanity again, packing concealer under her eyes.

"Purple is your power color," Andrea asserted. "We'll get you a Fitz blazer at the school store. For now, try this one." Andrea handed me a tan blazer. The word 'Legacy' was etched on the breast. I fingered the stitches, letting the string run over the pads of my fingers. The blazer stopped at my waist and she buttoned it closed.

"You were hiding that gorgeous body in those bulky clothes!" Andrea said. "You look amazing now! Look, Reggie," she ordered, never taking her eyes off me, obviously pleased with the work she did. Regina whipped around and her brown eyes widened.

"Gorge." She smiled sweetly.

"What are those? An eight?" Andrea gestured to my winter boots that were tossed haphazardly into the corner.

"Eight and a half," I answered.

She pulled out another pair of boots, identical to Regina's and said, "Try those on. They are last year's Prada, but no one will notice."

I slipped my foot inside and zipped the boot up my calf. It felt like a little slice of heaven.

"Now," Andrea flopped back on Regina's bed again, "you look like one of us."

I ran my hands over the thick cotton dress. It stuck to my curves in all the right places. I turned around in Regina's floor length mirror and didn't recognize myself in something so tight. Andrea was right, I felt powerful. I felt like I could blend in with everyone else.

"Mind my pillows," Regina called to the both of us as I threw myself back onto her bed.

Andrea's heeled boots click-clacked on the campus' cobblestone. She carefully maneuvered around the cracks and made the calculated movements look effortless. She didn't look down once as if the entire world were her runway. Dark aviator sunglasses shielded her eyes, and I couldn't tell where she was looking. I hoped she wasn't watching me watch her.

Regina was glued to her iPhone. Her thumbs flew across the screen so quickly. She blushed at whatever she was reading and I wondered how many messages she got like that a day. How many guys fawned over Regina Fitzgerald, heiress to the Fitzgerald throne?

I tried not to get caught up in my thoughts and keep up with the both of them. I didn't want to crease Regina's Prada boots as I scurried behind them on the way to breakfast.

Several girls stopped and let Regina and Andrea pass as the three of us moved through the clusters of students on campus. Just a few hours ago the whole place was empty and regal, and now, it was full of life and a sea of color.

Cackles of laughter cut through the silence in the courtyard, whipping between buildings. I caught bits and pieces of conversations as people herded in one direction, inside. Some were discussing homework and others the latest episode of a reality TV show that came on a channel I couldn't afford at home. Others were complimented on shoes or accessories with designer names, and staggering prices were thrown around like Frisbees.

And everyone else who wasn't talking was wondering who the hell I was. I tucked my hair behind my ear and tried to keep up with Regina and Andrea as they bounced up the steps into another brick building.

"This is the caf," Andrea shouted over the conversations that magnified once we were inside. It reminded me of the cafeteria in my community college, except there was no fighting or screaming. People stood around, some sitting on tabletops of round tables, engaged in polite conversation, not screaming into cell phones or at each other.

Flyers were taped around the room of upcoming social activities, concerts, and lectures. Floor-length posters were plastered on the walls of prominent African-Americans. The black and white photographs of Dr. Martin Luther King Jr., Malcolm X, Jackie Robinson, and countless others all bore the same message in white block letters: BLACK EXCELLENCE. This was their mantra. This was what they believed in. I could smell the money in the room.

When the three of us walked toward the interior of the room, it seemed like the music stopped. I winced, noticing the stares and hushed whispers between everyone. Regina walked ahead, like nothing had changed in the atmosphere. She fell into the arms of a tall, broad-chested guy who seemed more than happy to have her there. The two of them spoke for a few seconds before parting. He watched her butt as she walked away, pushing his hands into the pockets of his Dockers.

"We usually sit there, in front of the Starbucks." Andrea looped her arm in mine as we passed a group of girls who had a serious eye problem. No one else seemed to notice. Andrea stopped at a table that, coincidentally, had three open seats. I took a look around and to my surprise Jeffrey was sitting there, biting into a cinnamon donut just as the three of us approached the table. He did a dramatic double take, mid-chew, when he recognized me. The chewed bit of donut dropped on the table and rolled into the lap of another girl, who squealed in disgust.

"Ew, Jeff!" She laughed, tossing the piece back toward him. It hit him on the chest then dropped back on the table.

"Your mother never taught you to chew?" The light skinned girl flipped her long braids over her shoulder and rolled her enormous green eyes. Her face was covered in too much foundation like she dipped her face into a pie.

"Pipe down, Corrine," Andrea ordered. "Everyone this is—"

"Raevyn Elizabeth Jones." Jeffrey's voice was airy. He took another bite of his donut, neglecting to wipe the cinnamon flakes that had fallen on his sweater.

"Thanks for Kanye-ing her introduction." Regina flopped down into an empty seat beside Jeffrey. "She's Brooke's replacement. You two know each other?"

Before Jeffrey could answer, she pulled out a tissue from her purse, dabbing at the mess on his sweater.

"Corrine Williams of Williams and Associates in Chicago," Green Eyes said. "Pleasure to meet you, Raevyn."

"She hates her middle name," Andrea whispered and pulled me toward the other two empty seats. "So don't ask about it." I nodded while she practically pushed me down in a seat next to her. "You obviously already know Jeffrey." Andrea drew his name out and turned her nose up in his direction. "And now Corrine Rayne."

Corrine's eyes flashed a dark green. Her lip trembled, only for a millisecond, in animosity.

Andrea didn't notice and continued, "The rudeness here is Brandon Harper Delaney of the Wilson Funeral Home in Houston." She gestured to a dark skinned guy on the other side of Jeffrey. He waved in my direction, never looking up from his book. A red bow tie was knotted at his neck, which complemented the red and navy paisley square cloth that hung out of his blazer pocket. Did everyone here drop out of a catalog?

"He's Jeffrey's roommate and a complete book nerd," Andrea finished.

He flipped a middle finger in her direction.

"We are the only people you need to know here." Corrine smiled, while sipping on an iced coffee. Corrine, Andrea, and Regina got up from the table at the same time, linked their arms together, and walked away.

What was I supposed to do now?

"Hungry?" Jeff asked from across the table. He pushed his glasses on the bridge of his nose.

"There are omelettes in that corner." He pointed to a line that snaked around the room. "You gotta get here early for those. Gary's the best. There's hot food like pancakes, eggs, bacon, and that kinda stuff in the other corner. A la carte food there." He pointed to a lonely stand a couple feet away. "And then, there's always coffee." He nodded his head at the bustling Starbucks ahead.

"Lunch and dinner are pretty much the same set up," Jeffrey explained with a bored tone. He dipped his head as if someone nearby would be eavesdropping. "I wish we had a McDonald's in here."

"You eat McDonald's?" I scoffed. I couldn't imagine these kids eating anything that wasn't farm raised, unprocessed, or organic.

"Brandon and I," Jeffrey started under his breath, "used to drive all the way downtown to get a twenty piece. Guilty pleasure." He shrugged. Maybe Jeffrey wasn't a stuck up brat like I first imagined.

"Something about that artificial chicken..." Brandon commented, rubbing his stomach. The two of them cracked up together. "Man, we haven't done that in a long time."

My grumbling stomach forced me to make a decision, and after much contemplation, I picked the place with the least traffic, the a la carte tray. I didn't want anyone to step on Regina's Prada shoes. I could never pay her back if they got messed up.

When I got back to the table, only Jeffrey and Brandon were still there. Where was Regina?

"I see you're acclimating well." Jeffrey chewed an apple. "You're fitting right in." His words were laced with something. Sarcasm? I couldn't tell. A smirk toyed at the corners of his mouth and his eyes played tug-of-war with mine. He glanced over at Brandon, who wasn't paying us any attention, before whispering, "I liked the jeans better."

I pretended to tuck an unruly coil of hair behind my ear to hide my smile. I suppressed the heat rushing to my face. I had to concentrate on something else to keep from blushing. I glanced around at the other girls who were all wearing a variation of the same outfit as Regina, Andrea, and I. Most wore blazers and boots or sweater leggings and Uggs. Everyone seemed to have a standard B. W. Fitz blazer, advertising their legacy. A few white and pale yellow blazers were sprinkled amongst the sea of tan, maroon, and black ones.

"What do the different colors mean?" I whispered to Jeffrey before thinking twice.

He eyed me before answering. "Black and maroon are the Fitz colors. Yellow blazers are for upperclassmen in the honors program and white blazers are for senior honors. Those are the really smart kids. The doctors, the engineers, the Brandon's." He nudged Brandon who finally looked up from his huge textbook.

"They are the overachievers," Brandon said in a nasally voice. He flashed his metallic smile at me. Braces. He was still handsome, if nerds were your thing. "I'll be one, one day," he said airily, eyeing a guy who drifted past us in a white blazer, with his nose, literally, in the air.

To me, everyone here was an overachiever. They were all what the posters prompted them to be—Black Excellence.

And here I was, in someone else's clothes, attempting to blend.

After a long while, we flooded out of the cafeteria and across the courtyard to a white stone building with the striking gold roof. The conversations died as soon as we reached the steps.

I passed under the sculpted columns and the oak French doors opened to a carpeted burgundy sanctuary. The hundreds of cushioned pews slanted welcomingly into each other. I tried not to act like a tourist, but the high vaulted ceilings and tall stained glass windows were impeccable.

School officials cloaked in sweeping burgundy robes sat in the pulpit, waiting patiently, as the students filed in. I noticed Miss Tanner first. She looked like a floating head in the billowing robe. Regina snuck her arm through mine and led me directly to the front. I could feel everyone's eyes glued to my back. No one said anything but I could practically hear minds churning, wondering, *Who's the new girl?*

Regina, Andrea, and Corrine glided up the center aisle smiling at dozens of people, waving and winking. They were powerful. They were popular. They were the 'it' girls, I could tell, and my roommate was the head of the pack.

Once everyone was settled in, an elderly man crept to the microphone. The crowd continued to rustle, whispering, 'Good morning's' or 'Love your boots!' But as soon as he cleared his throat an eerie silence swept the room.

"Good morning, scholars." He addressed the mass of students with smiling eyes. His oval shaped glasses threatened to jump off the edge of his nose. From where we were seated, I could see that Parkinson's disease would soon overtake his body. He gripped the sides of the podium for balance and began speaking on the blessings that each new day brings.

Automatically, my heart softened. He reminded me of my grandfather. I'd only seen pictures of him, particularly one picture, in his younger days, where he was holding me. He must have said something funny because the both of us were laughing, our emotions frozen in time. I'd only seen that picture a couple of times, when mom was feeling well enough to decorate for Christmas, but the image of his smiling face always stuck with me.

"Good morning, headmaster Randolph," everyone answered in a singsong manner.

"As many of you know, Brooke Wheeler had an unfortunate emergency and could not stay to finish the semester." His voice crackled. He cleared his throat and continued.

"It is my understanding that we have a new pupil." He searched the crowd fervently and finally his eyes settled and locked on mine. My heart stopped. A few people followed his gaze and I heard everyone shift in my direction. I slouched in my seat, praying that I would melt through the floor. *Please don't make me introduce myself,* I begged.

"Please welcome Miss Raevyn Elizabeth Jones to our campus. I hope you will feel right at home here." I made sure to smile at Miss Tanner who looked like she'd regurgitate the little she probably ate for breakfast that morning.

Corrine winked and grabbed my hand. "You'll be fine," she whispered. I guessed she could hear my heartbeat pumping in surround sound.

Headmaster Randolph continued on about the new security updates and several other announcements concerning campus safety. Once he finished talking, everyone rose in one swift motion, like a choir. Regina nearly snatched me out of my seat when I was late in standing. Three monitors descended from the ceiling and a muffled audio snaked through the speakers along the ends of the aisles.

Then, everyone, all at once, began to recite the same words. I recognized the voice immediately. It was the end of Dr. Martin Luther King Jr.'s 'I Have a Dream Speech.' I looked through my hair at Corrine who was plucking the skin from her cuticles while mouthing the words and then over at Regina, who was texting on her iPhone by her side, never missing a word either. She looked over at me then pointed to the monitors.

"Follow along," she mouthed.

After the speech, we all filed out of the church and into the blistering cold once again. Some students hung around to chat with their friends, while others beat it across campus.

I just followed the crowd until Corrine caught up to me. "So what's your first class?"

"Uh." I racked my brain to remember the schedule that was probably still up on my laptop. Why didn't I print it?

"Raevyn!" Jeffrey shuffled over. "I tried to catch you before you ran off. You dropped this." He pulled a folded paper from his pants pocket.

Corrine snatched it before me. "Aframhis." She smirked. "You'd better hope it's not with Professor Carmichael."

"Oooh." Regina walked up arm-in-arm with Andrea. She wiggled her fingers to a freakishly tall, handsome guy who lingered a little too long before finally walking away. I saw Jeffrey grimace out of the corner of my eye.

"Aframhis," she repeated the same words like Corrine. "That's going to kick your ass."

"What?" I took the paper from Corrine. My first class was African American History. "Shouldn't be that hard," I mumbled.

"You keep thinking that." Andrea lowered her dark shades, revealing her enticing eyes. "Especially if you have Carmichael."

The three of them walked away.

"And if I don't?" I called after them.

"It'll still kick your ass," Regina declared over her shoulder. "Meet us at the table at lunch." I realized Regina only spoke in demands.

"See ya!" Corrine waved, smiling at me like I was her child and it was my first day of kindergarten. I thought her hand would fly off her wrist.

"See ya," I mumbled, taking off in the other direction.

"You're this way." Jeffrey pointed over his shoulder. I almost forgot he was standing there.

"Thanks for my schedule." I slid the paper in my pocket. "I totally forgot to print it."

"It's okay," he said, falling into step next to me. "I remember how it was on my first day. I was scared out of my mind. This place can be really intense."

Intense wasn't the word I was thinking. B. W. Fitz was terrifying.

As we passed crowds of people, Jeffrey stopped and held two-second conversations with almost everyone. He'd ask about the person's parents or their family business. He would ask how their schoolwork was going or if they'd gotten started on a project or their senior thesis. He was one of those guys that had no close friends, but everyone else considered him their best friend.

"You know everyone," I commented, trying not to admire his genuine smile or his or his unblemished chocolate skin.

"What can I say?" He shrugged, looking down at me through his glasses. For a millisecond it felt like this morning—just the two of us, walking through the empty campus, only the sound of our footsteps aligned with each other.

"What's up with this Carmichael guy?" I asked, hugging myself. I made a mental note that I would need a thicker coat if I wanted to last another day in Ohio without freezing to death.

"He's just a hard ass." Jeffrey flexed his gloved hand. "He's one of those professors that grade hard, no curves whatsoever, so don't expect one. Don't miss a class, and don't challenge him, or he'll try to fail you every chance he gets."

I gulped. "Are you in this class?"

"I have him on Tuesdays and Thursdays," he answered. "I can try and help you catch up as much as possible."

We both approached a building that looked identical to a dungeon. It was the only building on campus, besides the church, that wasn't encased in brick. The steps retreated downwards into the structure and our footsteps echoed hauntingly against the concrete walls.

"This is where we have class?" I asked, pulling my coat tighter around myself. The farther we went, the colder it got.

"This was the first building built on this campus." Jeffrey lowered his voice as we closed in on the only door on the bottom level. Inside, I could see a few students already sitting down, their noses crammed in their books.

"Carmichael refuses to move into a newer building. He's stubborn."

"He sounds like an asshole," I said matter-of-factly.

Jeffrey's eyes popped like he never heard someone curse before.

"What?" I asked.

"No one has ever called me an asshole before...at least not to my face."

I dug my nails into my palms. Of course the first time I meet my professor, a notoriously harsh professor at that, I would call him an asshole. Jeffrey gave me the most apologetic look when Professor Carmichael cut in again.

"Miss Jones, I presume?" His words dripped with disdain.

I turned and gave him the toothiest grin. "Yes, sir. Raevyn Elizabeth Jones." I held my hand out but he made a point not to shake it. Instead, he raised a mug to his lips taking a loud, disgusting slurp from it. I took in his beady eyes and bushy eyebrows, coupled with his pointy nose. You had to be an asshole with a face like that. I didn't think it was such an unfair assumption to make.

"Of?" His dark, beady eyes darted between mine. His surgically enhanced pointy nose rested on the rim.

"Excuse me?" I asked.

"Your lineage." Jeffrey tried to cough the words through his fist.

"Oh!" I tried to mimic Regina's smile. "Jones Funeral Home in Atlanta."

For a while he didn't speak and the walls seemed to be closing in around us. He just stood there as if he were deciding whether to pass or fail me on the spot.

"Interesting," he finally said, glowering between both Jeffery and I. "Miss Jones, inside." He nodded toward the door and I darted around him.

"Mr. Donnelly, aren't you supposed to be across campus by now?" He lifted his sleeve revealing a black Movado watch, identical to the one Antoine used to wear. Although I'm sure Professor Carmichael paid for his. "You have about three minutes before your own class begins."

"I know, sir. I was just walking Miss Jones. It's her first day—"

"Well, she seems to have found it pretty successfully, wouldn't you think?"

"Yes, sir." Jeffrey gave me another regretful look before turning on the spot and sprinting in the opposite direction.

"In," Professor Carmichael ordered without turning around. I scrambled inside and took the seat closest to the door. I wanted to get this over with as soon as possible and stay far away from Professor Asshole.

My first day at Benjamin Wallace Fitzgerald didn't go as smoothly as I thought it would. Regina's designer clothes didn't help me become another face in a crowd either. I was like graffiti on a police station. I was that moment in your favorite song where the music skips. I was the pesky stain on your favorite blouse.

Everyone noticed me.

I was incapable of blending no matter how hard I tried. As the day went on I felt more and more like an outsider. Between my meeting with Miss Tanner, Professor Carmichael and the unwelcoming stares, I wasn't too excited about spending the next couple of years here.

I flopped down on my bed around dinnertime and let my syllabi, the assigned readings, and the homework that was due 'as soon as possible since I missed so much of the semester' fall to the floor. I'd never been too much of a crier, but I could feel myself becoming more and more overwhelmed. I wasn't cut out to do this. I wasn't a prissy college girl who takes honors classes, wears name brands, and expensive perfume.

All I wanted to do was be with Antoine. My father hid my cell phone before we left Maryland but I'd do anything to hear his voice right now. I grabbed a pillow, pushed it on my face and let out a hellish scream until my throat burned, but it didn't help. I was about to try again when Regina popped her head into my doorway.

"How was your first day?" She flicked her fingers across the screen of her iPhone, never looking up. A bolt of envy shot through me. I bet her cell phone never got taken away. I bet Regina got everything she wanted.

"Are you always attached to that thing?" I sneered and picked up the papers nearest me.

"Always." She ignored my attitude and smiled while picking up my African American History syllabus. "How was this?"

"I'd rather go to hell." I sorted out the papers into three piles: syllabi, homework, and stuff to buy. I dropped my head in my hands feeling a massive headache brewing. Per the guidelines, I had to maintain a 3.5 GPA *and* my dad ordered me to hold down an on-campus job. Lovely.

"Let me see," Regina said, picking up my 'stuff to buy' pile. She flipped through the stacks of papers. "I still have some of these books from last year. I'll look on the bookcase. We can hit the school store for the rest of this." She tossed the pile back at me nonchalantly and backed out of the room.

Did she not see the prices on that list? I didn't have money to purchase a $200 calculus book. Minutes later, returned with an armful of books.

"This should do it, right?" She dropped the books on my bed and referenced the list again. "Shit, you still need Carmichael's books." She clicked her nail against her teeth.

"You still helped me out a lot."

"And you still need a Fitz blazer," she reminded me.

I looked down at hers, running my fingers over the word 'Legacy' again. "Oh, I don't know. I can manage with the clothes I have." I shrugged. I remembered my bulky sweater and Technicolor jeans. If I still managed to stick out in Regina's clothes, I'd be a walking circus attraction tomorrow. Still, I had no choice.

"Why are you Southerners so damn frugal?" She sighed. "You should have seen the fight Brandon put up last year. Now look at him." She slapped her hands on her thighs. "Listen, I'll pay for it," she offered. "Let us dress you."

I scoffed. "Us?"

"Andrea and I," she said. "Oh and Corrine." She swatted at her name like it was an annoying gnat. "You're going to be the Belle of the Fitzgerald ball."

Regina hit a couple buttons on her phone and began to chat away with both Corrine and Andrea, closing my bedroom door behind her before I even got a chance to get another word in. Why did I get the feeling that this wouldn't go well?

The whole world around me moved in slow motion.

The clock on the dash read 6:37 p.m., just before the seatbelt grabbed my throat. I heard Antoine scream for me, his hands flew frantically, trying to gain control of the car, but it was too late. The cash rained around us, catapulting this way and that, blocking his view of the road. The steering wheel jerked demonically like someone else was driving.

We fishtailed then whipped in the opposite direction. Chunks of gravel jumped, popping against the windshield.

Antoine stomped on the brake. Our tires skid across the road, smoke billowed in the air, and then it felt like we were flying.

My stomach rose then dropped, and before I could scream, before I realized what was happening, my mouth collided with the dashboard when the car finally slammed to a stop.

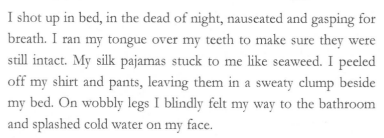

I shot up in bed, in the dead of night, nauseated and gasping for breath. I ran my tongue over my teeth to make sure they were still intact. My silk pajamas stuck to me like seaweed. I peeled off my shirt and pants, leaving them in a sweaty clump beside my bed. On wobbly legs I blindly felt my way to the bathroom and splashed cold water on my face.

I was safe.

"You're okay, Rae," I said to myself before melting to the floor. The icy marble cooled my body. It had been nearly six months since the accident, but the memory stuck with me, transforming my dreams into nightmares.

My heart began to beat at a normal pace. I slipped Antoine's favorite Incredible Hulk T-shirt over my head, and although he was miles away, my heart still longed for him.

It had been almost two weeks at B. W. Fitz, and I was beginning to get into the swing of things, and by swing of things, I meant I wasn't arriving thirty minutes late to my classes anymore. I printed off a campus map from the school website and referenced that when I got turned around since every building was identical. I even got about half of the Dream speech memorized.

Blending hadn't become any easier, but I wasn't the campus spectacle anymore either. Regina and Andrea dressed me everyday like their very own Old Navy mannequin. They quizzed me on labels and brand names every chance they got; stopping random people on campus, pointing to their bag or their shoes. Some brands were easy to identify because of their pretentious logos. There were tons of things I couldn't pronounce, the shoes weren't any easier to walk in, and the dresses weren't getting any looser. But, things were a tad better. Only a tad. At least I was blending like my father wanted me to. I hadn't got into any trouble. I hadn't received any harassing emails from Miss Tanner about my grades and nothing was burned down yet.

But, I longed for home. I wanted to be back with my own friends. I wanted to be home where people were welcoming and didn't expect your full name when you were introduced. I was accepted at home. Here, I was completely out of my element.

My new wardrobe made me another face in the crowd, but I still felt like the same girl I was on my first day—the outsider.

My mouth felt like I swallowed a fistful of cotton balls. I crept through the living room, and into the hallway, careful not to let the suite door slam behind me. I didn't want to wake Regina. She was a light sleeper. I received several 'try to keep it down' notes on my door while I studied, which was usually late at night with music on its lowest setting. Still, it was too loud for princess Regina. I twisted the handle around and the door closed without a sound.

The dim lights casted haunting shadows in the hallway. The floors creaked as I traveled downstairs. Overhead, an industrial light blinked on automatically when I entered the kitchen. I pulled a glass from the cabinet and filled it with water. Once I downed the glass I left the cup in the sink and the lights blinked off when I left.

Then, I heard faint voices like whispers of conversation coming from the phone room. Who would be chatting so late? The phone room, diagonal from the kitchen, was literally the size of a box with a landline for people like me with no personal phones to use. It was normally empty because every normal person had a cell phone nowadays. Mrs. Potts refused to turn it into an on-the-go phone charging station. She said it kept the old charm of the dormitory.

I crept closer to the door and realized more than one voice was cutting into each other. This was an argument.

"Are you sure she was sleeping when you left?" someone asked.

"Yes, quit asking me that!" someone else hissed.

"So, what are we going to do? She can't come back here."

"Why not?" a third person asked. "You're the only one that has a problem with her."

"Corrine, spare me." I knew that condescending voice from anywhere. That was Andrea. "You have a problem with the bitch, too."

"Yeah, but she's my best friend," Corrine whined.

"She can't come back, you're right." I assumed the last voice was Regina's. It was barely above a whisper. "The semester is almost over. That leaves us winter break to figure this out."

"I'm going to bed." Andrea yawned. "I have an Econ pre-final tomorrow that I can't fail messing around with y'all."

While they argued a bit more, I slipped past the room unnoticed and darted up the stairs. A million questions invaded my brain. Was I the *she* they spoke about? Were they trying to stop *me* from coming back next semester? Could they do that? Why? Why would they do that? Why waste all their time and money quizzing me on name brands and itchy fabrics if they just wanted me to leave? Did Miss Tanner set this up? That woman just wouldn't quit.

My gut reaction was to get mad, but instead, dread filled my veins. Everyone thought I was a legacy. They thought if I got kicked out I could just go back to my home in Atlanta and attend some other college. They didn't know this was my last shot. I had to ace every test and complete every assignment because I had to stay at B. W. Fitz. I had nowhere else to go. I realized that I had to act like a legacy.

I can't believe I just said that, I thought.

I slipped back under my covers just as I heard Regina's bedroom door open and click closed. I didn't know what would happen next, but I knew it wouldn't be good.

The next morning at breakfast, everything seemed normal. Brandon's nose was glued to the crack of an Anatomy book, and Regina was speed texting. Andrea flipped through Vogue magazine, turning her nose up at some celebrity's fashion choices, or dog-earing a page she approved of.

"Say what you want about those Kardashians," she announced, sipping on a Frappuccino, "but they are fabulous." Her dark lipstick left a stain on her coffee cup. As usual, her skin was flawless. She didn't look like she was up at 3 a.m. planning my demise.

Weirdly, Jeffrey hadn't arrived yet. He was never late. I looked around the cafeteria at the clusters of people and couldn't spot him. I had to tell him what I heard last night. Maybe he could help me make sense of everything. Maybe I was overreacting and I wasn't the girl they were talking about. If I wasn't, then who was?

"Brandon, did you see Jeffrey this morning?" I asked.

Regina narrowed her eyes at me before Brandon answered, "Yeah, he was dressed when I left."

"He's just never late," I commented. "Just seems weird." I craned my neck towards the door but I couldn't see over the throngs of people who crowded the entrance.

"Sounds exactly like Jeffrey to me." Regina shrugged. "He'll be here."

Just then, Corrine clambered over. Her braids twisted into a sloppy bun. She had on her usual maroon Legacy blazer with a fitted white V-neck FITZ T-shirt paired with black sweater leggings that hugged her hips. Her butt curved into a tight bubble. Her tall tan Uggs clunked against the floor as she approached. For once she didn't have any make-up on and I noticed dark freckles sprinkled along the bridge of her nose and the balls of her cheeks. Corrine looked pretty. She looked normal like someone I could possibly be friends with outside of here.

"Well, look what the cat drug in," Andrea murmured without looking up from her magazine. "Long night, Corrine?"

She plopped down at the table, ignoring Andrea's teasing. She dropped her oversized YSL tote bag to the floor and fished out what looked like a study guide. She flipped her wrist around, glancing at her Michael Kors watch and then studying the door. She must have noticed Jeffrey was late too.

"I didn't know you had freckles." Brandon took a long look at Corrine. Her cheeks flushed a bright pink, and before any of us could comment, Jeffrey approached.

"Bow to me," he exclaimed, straightening his lavender bowtie. He scrambled over to an open seat beside me and began digging around in his Ferragamo messenger bag.

"I got us invitations to *the* most exclusive Christmas ball," he bragged, pulling out several wax-sealed envelopes.

"You didn't!" Regina squealed in disbelief.

"Don't play around, Jeffrey." Andrea cut her eyes at him. Jeffrey's announcement even caused Brandon to look up from his book.

"The Mason Christmas Ball?" Corrine looked down at Jeffrey hungrily.

"Don't be ridiculous." Andrea declared. "Those invitations are for seniors. We couldn't get in if we tried."

"*The* Mason Christmas Ball," Jeffrey confirmed for the salivating crowd.

Regina and Andrea exchanged glances that looked like they were about to either scream or pee on themselves.

"How did you do that?" Brandon asked, snatching an envelope from Jeffrey and running his hand under the seal.

"There are perks for being the best assistant to the dean of students," he answered knowingly. He passed out five envelopes. I quickly realized there wasn't one for me. I hoped everyone would be too busy tearing into their own invitations to notice.

"Sorry," he whispered above the excited chatter. "I could only get five."

I could feel Regina's eyes on me. "It's okay." I shrugged. "I have way too much work to do anyway." Suddenly, I felt flushed. "I hope you guys have fun."

"Maybe I can get a plus one?" Jeffrey guessed.

"It seems pretty exclusive from the looks of it."

"At least let me try." His hand landed softly on top of mine. I was sure it was a mistake or just a natural reaction to make me feel better. He wasn't purposefully trying to make me internally combust. I snatched my hand away, stuffing it under my leg, trying my best to ignore the electric sensation that zipped through me.

"We have to go shopping today!" Corrine shrilled. "I saw this amazing backless Valentino jumpsuit that would look so good on me."

"A jumpsuit? Really? For the Mason ball?" Brandon slanted his eyes at Corrine.

"I get out of my final at six. We could get to the city by six thirty," Andrea confirmed, typing on her iPhone. "Vincent's usually closes at seven, but maybe Daddy can get him to keep it open a little while longer just for us, you know? Vincent's son is trying to be a singer, I'm sure he will do it," she rambled on.

"I said Valentino, not Forever 21." Corrine rolled her eyes at Brandon.

"Are you coming?" Regina asked, looking up at me with ice in her eyes. I was quite sure she heard the conversation Jeffrey and I shared. Everyone stopped his or her own side conversations and finally noticed my lack of an invitation.

"I get out of French around six-thirty. I don't think I would be able to make it anyway." I answered. "You guys can go ahead without me, right?"

The air grew sparse. I gathered my things and Corrine gave me a soft, apologetic smile. I hoped Jeffrey could get another invitation, but something told me it was wishful thinking.

"I'll see you guys at lunch," I announced, before walking away, attempting to convince myself that I didn't care.

I didn't know why French was called the love language. The last thing I wanted to do, when I was in French class, was fall in love. Studying French made me want to pull every strand of my hair out of my head one by one. I was doing pretty well in it, only because the guy that sat beside me was some kind of French genius and also happened to be left-handed. He turned his paper upside down to write which meant I didn't even have to lean over too far to ace my exams. Thank God for oblivious lefties.

Professor Bonhomme droned on about past and present tense participles, and now more than ever before, I wished I had a cell phone. I could text someone or at the very least play a mind numbing game. I rested my chin on my hand. Out of the window, small flecks of snow were beginning to float gracefully to the ground. I noticed a tiny light flashing in my direction against the blackness of the evening sky.

I turned around, realizing Leftie was trying to get my attention. He made texting motions with his phone.

He mouthed, "What's your number?"

Here's another thing I'd have to get used to at B. W. Fitz— the attention. Back home, I was Antoine's girl and everyone knew that. I was off-limits. Guys didn't ask for my number or walk me to my class because they would have to deal with either Wade, Antoine's best friend, or Antoine himself, if he ever found out. And nobody ever wanted to deal with Antoine directly. Nobody.

I never noticed how cute Leftie actually was. I guessed I was too busy copying off his paper. He just made it so easy.

Leftie reminded me of Antoine. He didn't wear stuffy bow ties or fitted pants like most of the guys. He wasn't flashy and over the top. Leftie was just a regular guy and I liked that.

"I don't have one," I admitted.

He gave me a sarcastic look and I knew I should have just said I lost it. I wouldn't have believed me either.

He flipped one of his wandering dreadlocks back into place. "If you didn't want me to text you, you could have just told me that."

"No, I really don't have a phone."

He leaned closer to me and I got a whiff of his familiar Hugo Boss cologne, Antoine's favorite. I tried not to get swept up in his fragrance when he asked, "Where are you from? Outer space?"

"Yeah," I whispered back. "Venus."

"Miss Jones," Professor Bonhomme bellowed. I didn't realize he stopped speaking and was staring directly at Leftie and me. "Perhaps you two should take your love connection outside?" He crossed his meaty arms over his chest, glaring at the two of us. I glanced between Professor Bonhomme, Leftie, who had already begun packing his bags, and the rest of the class who refused to make eye contact. Was he really kicking me out of class?

"After you, mademoiselle," Leftie said, choking back a laugh. I gathered all my things, slipped past my professor, and followed Leftie outside. I hadn't gotten sent out of class since twelfth grade. My dad would be livid if he were here.

"So tell me, Raevyn Elizabeth Jones, how's life on Venus?" Leftie zipped up his NorthFace jacket. The temperature dropped drastically since lunch.

"Cold," I answered, laughing lightly. "And you are?"

"Oh, come on." He dramatically brought his hand over his heart like he'd been shot. "You've sat beside me for weeks and you don't even know my name?"

I gave him a sheepish grin.

"It's Dre, well, Andre Pierre Mouton from New Orleans, Louisiana."

I made a mental note that he didn't say his legacy. Was he a scholarship student?

"You're Creole." I wagged my finger at him. "That's why you're so good at French."

"Guilty." He smiled, looking down at his feet. "You're not very good at it so it's a good thing I'm also ambidextrous."

I stopped in my tracks. "You knew this whole time?"

"Relax." He laughed at the mortified look on my face. "I never said I minded."

"So, you're not even left handed?"

"I'm naturally right handed."

"I'm really sorry, Andre," I offered. "I'm just *so* terrible at French."

"You don't have to apologize," he assured me. "I get it." When the silence between us amplified he asked, "Why don't you have a cell phone?"

"I just don't," I blurted. It seemed like the simplest answer. I didn't want to get into why and he didn't need to know why either.

"Then how am I supposed to contact you?"

"What?" I was stunned for the second time in all of five minutes.

"How am I supposed to take you out if I don't have your number?" He spoke slower this time, like I didn't hear him the first time. He took me by the hands and pulled me toward him. I felt his breath dance on my face.

Take me *out*? *Me*? I scrambled to think of something that Andrea would say. "I'm sure you'll figure something out." The heavens seemed to open up, saving me from making a bigger fool of myself. The wind began to pick up and the snow began to fall in bigger flakes.

"You'd better get inside, Mr. Mouton."

"Call me Dre," he instructed, while he pulled my glove off my hand. His full, soft lips graced the back of my hand. The warm gesture radiated through my body. I couldn't feel the cold anymore. Pterodactyls flapped around in my stomach. He looked up at me—while I tried to act like I wasn't about to faint—and said, "Goodnight, Miss Jones."

I watched Andre through the door until he blended in with the darkness. It felt like I was in a made for TV movie. I couldn't believe this was my life.

I rounded the corner, skipping towards the elevator bank when Mrs. Potts called out for me, putting a pin in my Disney princess fantasy. I turned in the opposite direction and noticed her gray hair poking out from the phone room. "Raevyn, is that you?" she called again.

"Yes, ma'am?"

"Phone's for you." The color drained out of her face when she placed the receiver in my hand. She cleared her throat. "I've, um, already accepted the charges."

"The…what?" Mrs. Potts scurried out of the room as I cradled the phone to my ear.

"Raevyn," Antoine spoke first, "I don't have much time." My hand trembled as I pressed the receiver to my ear. My throat felt like it was closing. I couldn't speak. I couldn't breathe. My knees collapsed under me.

"Bird?" he asked. "Are you there?"

"H-How did you get this number?" I stammered.

"Damn, I didn't think that would be the first thing we said to each other."

"I didn't mean it like that," I backtracked, telling my mind to slow down. It was reeling with thoughts. My heart was pumping with raw emotion—happiness, relief, and sadness all at the same time. Before I knew it, tears were popping from my eyes.

"God, Antoine, I missed you." I sobbed, wishing I could see him, wishing I could hold him. "It's been so hard without you."

"Don't cry, Bird." His voice softened. "I need you to be strong for me."

"Of course," I answered, taking a huge breath, attempting to settle down. "Of course I will."

"One minute," a recorded voice chimed in.

"Bird, I need you to listen to me," Antoine ordered. "You've got to get some money together to get me out of here."

"I gave Wade everything I had before I left. What'd he do with that?"

"It's not enough. Bird, I can't stay in here another day. You know I wouldn't ask if I didn't need it. It's killing me calling you like this." He sounded pitiful. I could only imagine what he was going through in there. In all the years I'd known Antoine he prided himself on never having to ask anyone for anything. I knew I was his last resort.

"Thirty seconds," the voice threatened.

"I need you, Bird."

"I start my job this week," I offered. "Maybe I can mail it to my dad?"

"No. Wade will come and get it from you. He'll take care of it."

"Wade? When?" My brain was moving in a million different directions.

"This weekend. Get as much as you can, Bird," he pleaded.

"Will I hear from you again?" My words collided like a traffic jam as I tried to beat the recorded voice that was now counting down the seconds.

"I'll always be able find you, little Bird," he assured me just before the line went dead.

I took the steps that night because I didn't want to run into Mrs. Potts on the way to the elevator. I felt like a zombie when I slugged back to my room. I had no idea how I would get any money to Antoine. I thought about selling my new clothes, but I didn't know if that would be enough. I slid my key into the lock, but the door creaked open. A pop song pumped out of the speakers. Bowls of pretzels and potato chips were scattered across the floor. I crushed an M&M with the sole of Regina's Prada boot. Would Regina notice these were gone if I sold them?

Regina, Corrine, and Andrea were sprawled out in the living room, having a full-on girls' night. The scent of nail polish remover assaulted me.

"There you are," Corrine shrieked when I closed the door behind me. She waved her fire engine red fingernails in my direction. "I just asked Regina when you were coming home. M&M?" She offered me the bowl.

"No, thanks," I answered, moving past the three of them.

"You really need a phone," Andrea commented. She swiped a line of red polish on her big toenail. Her tongue stuck out of her mouth while she concentrated. I stepped over her and twisted the doorknob to my room when she said, "What's your deal?"

She whipped the long bangs out of her eyes. Regina pressed a button on the sound system and the pop song slowly died out. "You've been acting bitchy since breakfast."

"Ah-greed," Regina conceded, eyeing me accusingly. "Is it about the Mason ball?"

"Jeffrey said he would try and get a plus one for you," Corrine explained, her angelic voice promising and sincere.

"It's not that," I admitted, trying to filter the irritation from my voice. I just wanted to be left alone. I had so many things running through my mind that I had actually forgotten all about the Mason ball. Between Jeffrey and Dre, now Antoine, I couldn't concentrate on this unnecessary conversation. I felt so heavy, like sand lined the pockets of my jeans. "I'm just dealing with a bunch of stuff."

"It's that ex, huh?" Andrea alleged. She rested her chin on her knee, slowly stroking another coat of paint on her big toe. "I bet he's on you something serious now that you're gone. That's just like a guy. Once you leave him alone for a while he comes crawling right back." She wiped the paint off her cuticles with a Q-tip but missed, smudging the paint on her nail. "This is why I pay people to do this," she mumbled, attacking her toe with an acetone soaked cotton ball.

"It's like guys have radar," Corrine added. "I don't get it."

"Was he good to you?" Regina's tone was serious, calculating. Everyone quieted down when she spoke. Her toes, with cotton balls weaved between them, were propped on the footrest of the La-Z-Boy. She tossed a few kernels of popcorn in my mouth and waited for my answer.

Antoine didn't have the squeakiest background, but he always made sure I was taken care of. If there was a stupid Christmas ball that I wanted to go to he'd make sure I had a ticket, that was for sure. If there was a subject I was struggling in, he'd make someone give me their homework or the answers to tests. He wasn't the best guy on paper, but he was *my* guy, and he needed me. I owed him everything.

I was going to be an accessory to robbery and Antoine took the whole rap for me. He didn't want me to end up in jail. My blood was all over that car too, but Antoine cut a deal and I got off scot-free.

Once I healed, my dad tossed me in a car and drove me across country, away from the only guy who loved me. I left him hanging when he needed me the most and I felt awful for that.

I realized I owed everything to Antoine. Nothing could stop me from helping him. Not even the miles my father tried to put between us. I didn't care what I had to do, even if that meant sticking out of the crowd and selling everything I owned.

"Very much so." I choked back tears and tried to keep my voice from wavering.

"Then take him back," Regina responded as if it was that easy. She pushed a button on the remote beside her and the room quickly filled with obnoxious music again. The three of them began chatting again like nothing had happened, as if I hadn't come into the room at all.

I met Dr. Rudd at the gymnasium after classes the next day. The snowfall from the previous night had turned into slush and the maintenance staff worked through the day to make sure the path was safely salted. My Burberry rain boots served me well during the slippery trek across campus. I didn't want to think about parting with them. Dr. Rudd was already there, waiting for me at the administrative desk. His soft eyes sparkled when he saw me enter through the automatic doors.

"Ah, Miss Jones." He pulled me in for an awkward hug. I hesitantly placed my arms around his pudgy frame. I didn't know him, but he seemed to know me very well. "I haven't seen you since you were just a little girl." He held his hand down to his knee. His brilliant smile pushed his chunky cheeks into his eyes.

"Really?" I pulled off my fur-lined Chanel hat. I plucked my hair out from its mashed state while he continued talking.

"Don't tell me you don't remember," he said crestfallen. "Eh, it was a long time ago. I guess you couldn't if you tried. When your father called me and told me you were coming to Fitz, I knew I had to take good care of you."

"I appreciate that, sir," I said, following him down a hallway lined with office doors. We reached one at the end of the hall. "You and my father went to school together?"

He scoffed. "Oh yeah. We pledged together, worked together." He tallied off on his stubby fingers. "Your dad was my best friend. He, uh…" he searched the ground. "He made me your godfather so you don't have to call me sir or nothin' like that."

"For real?"

He shrugged. His cheeks flushed like he was embarrassed and I started to feel bad for resisting his hug earlier.I didn't even know my dad had best friends besides the guys at the construction site he played poker with sometimes on weekends. Dr. Rudd's name never came up in our conversations about B. W. Fitz, or any conversations for that matter.

I wondered how many strings Dr. Rudd pulled for me to get into Fitz. Miss Tanner hadn't breathed a word to me since that fateful day weeks ago in her office. I wondered if she said anything to Dr. Rudd like she threatened and I wonder if he defended me.

"Anyway," he continued, putting a pin in my thoughts. "Your dad told me he wanted you to stay out of trouble. What better way than working?" He poked me playfully in the ribs. "You're required to work at least fifteen hours out of the week. Most students only work ten, but your dad insisted on more. You can work more if you want, but fifteen is your minimum. Your Daddy wanted you to work twenty, but I figured that was too much. You need time for some fun."

I rolled my eyes. *Of course he did.*

"It's my understanding Ralphie will have you doing administrative work and handling general upkeep, etcetera, etcetera."

"Easy enough." I shrugged.

Dr. Rudd smiled at me like he was seeing me for the first time. I guess he kind of was. "Sounds easy, but this place can get pretty busy." I worked at Target during Christmas season. I knew what busy looked like. I was pretty sure I could handle an on-campus gym.

When the door opened I tried not to look too shocked that Ralphie was a woman. Not just a regular woman, either. She was jacked like she ate, slept and breathed iron. Her abs looked like I could wash all of Regina's laundry twice over. *She* was the reason why the gym was so busy. No one was coming here to work out. I wondered if she got cold walking around the gym in only a sports bra and biker shorts. But if I had that body, I'd probably wear the same thing.

"Terry," she sung, embracing Dr. Rudd with a long hug. "So good to see you."

"I have your new employee." Dr. Rudd hooked his arm through mine and pulled me in.

She looked between the both of us. "Don't tell me this is Chuck's little girl." Ralphie studied me, a smile loitering on her full, pink lips. "You look just like your daddy."

"I get that all the time at home." I hugged myself, missing my dad. He had friends. Good friends that called him 'Chuck' and not Charles; friends who obviously remembered me from some time ago when I was a little girl. I had a godfather. What happened in those twenty years that passed since he'd been back to B. W. Fitz? Why didn't he stay? Why didn't he ever come back? More importantly, what was he running from?

"I'm Selena," she introduced herself, embracing me tightly. Her thick hair smelled like strawberries.

"Tell her why we call you Ralphie," Dr. Rudd suggested and tried to hold in his laughter. His double chin bounced in delight.

Selena rolled her eyes at him and leaned against her doorframe. "Your father and this nut," she started, pointing at Dr. Rudd who was now doubled over from laughing, "dared me to stick my tongue on the Fitz statue in our senior year. The only problem was it was a damn blizzard outside."

"And her tongue got stuck!" Dr. Rudd couldn't wait for Selena to get to the punch line. Tears streamed down his face. "Just like the little boy from *A Christmas Story*."

"They've been calling me Ralphie ever since," she finished, shrugging her shoulders. "It was many, many years ago."

"And still so damn funny," Dr. Rudd added, slapping Selena on the shoulder.

She pushed him away. "Don't you have something to do?" She took me by the shoulder and turned me away from him. "Let's go, doll. I'll show you around."

"Take care of my baby," Dr. Rudd called after us. I glanced back at him and he gave me a sweet smile; one like my father gave to me before I left. I wished I could hear his voice, but maybe I had a dad away from my dad now.

Ralphie, or Selena, led me around the four-story gym. The bottom floor was the pool area and the locker rooms. The second floor was the tennis and racquetball court. Above that was the main entrance, the third floor, with the administrative area, and the weight machines. Finally, on the fourth floor was the cardio area, equipped with brand new treadmills and Stairmasters, she explained. She taught Zumba and spinning classes on the weekends in the classrooms that were free to employees. I didn't need any more cardio because maneuvering around the gym was a workout in itself.

Selena gave me a copy of her master swipe key that granted me unlimited access to each floor. She also gave me a walkie-talkie like the rest of her administrative staff.

"We usually don't use these. But, if we get an influx of people and one place needs back up, we'll just walkie the group and see who is available."

"Got it." I clipped the device to my belt loop.

"I make the schedules. I email it to you every Sunday at the beginning of the week. Or I can text you your shifts if that's easier. Terry said you need fifteen hours a week, right?"

I nodded. "I put you on for this Friday. When you get here, just come see me and I'll start you off with something simple. The uniform is a white FITZ shirt and blue pants."

"I'll have to get some pants." I made a mental note.

"There are some in Vincent's downtown," she suggested. "That's where all you cool kids shop, right?"

"Vincent's, right." I smiled.

"See you Friday," Selena said, pulling me in for another hug, before heading back onto the weight room floor.

Friday morning Mrs. Potts was standing in the foyer like she'd been waiting for me to show up. I stepped off the elevator and she scurried over like she was pretending to catch it too. I knew better. I had been successfully avoiding her ever since I got the call from Antoine. I knew she wanted to talk about it. She wanted to know who it was.

"'Morning, Raevyn," she said cheerfully, taking a sip of her coffee. Her slippers scratched against the hardwood while I tried to move around her.

"Good morning, Mrs. Potts," I replied dryly. She stepped in my direction, and again in the opposite direction like we were waltzing. Except, I never asked her to be my partner and there wasn't any classical music playing. I held her shoulders and whipped around, putting my back toward the emergency exit. Two consecutive beeps sounded. I looked over and the exit sign flashed green.

Did I do that?

"Raevyn," Mrs. Potts started, snapping me back to reality. Maybe I was seeing things. "I need to talk to you when you have a chance." She moved her foot around in a circle on the elevator floor. "About the other night…the phone call."

"Right," I replied, taking an exacting look at the exit sign. Red. The annoying buzzing sound continued. I discreetly threw my hip in that direction and the door expelled two soft beeps. Green. No buzzing. I had a key to the exit door? How?

Mrs. Potts leaned out of the elevator door, and I threw myself inside, blocking her view. I was dangerously close to her; so close I could count the moles on her face. "I have class until five, then I work at the gym until close. If you're still up I can stop by after?"

She stumbled backwards. "Maybe sometime this weekend," she countered. I nodded in response and finally, the elevator doors slid shut.

I fished my gym key out the front pocket of my purse. I waved it in front of the emergency exit and again, like last time, two beeps announced that I could safely exit. I pressed the handle on the door slowly, wincing, hoping the alarm wouldn't sound. It didn't. I stepped outside and the door slammed shut behind me. Before anyone could see me, I darted up the hill and towards the cafeteria grinning from ear to ear. Selena not only copied her master key to the gym, she copied her master key to the entire school! I slowed to a stop once the idea dropped into my brain. This was exactly what I needed to help Antoine and it wouldn't involve me selling my clothes. I was one step closer.

***

Selena was bench-pressing an enormous bar when I walked in that night. I didn't see a spotter in sight. This woman was an Amazon. She noticed me in the mirror when I approached her apprehensively.

I dropped my bag. "Do you need help with that?"

She replaced the weight and exhaled in a short, sharp breath. "With those chicken arms?" she teased, pinching my arm through my coat. *My chicken arms could lay people out*, I thought to myself. Selena didn't know that side of me. I wanted to let her continue to think I had 'chicken arms'.

She wiped down the machine, and a slew of guys were no longer paying attention to their weights. I thought one guy would pass out from concentrating on Selena's ass so hard. You'd think he had X-ray vision.

"Let's get you started." She winked at me.

She and I walked downstairs through the pool level and into the locker rooms. The chlorine smell took my breath away.

"Most people don't work out on Friday nights," she explained. "I wanted your first night to be pretty easy."

We passed the deep end of the pool and she opened the door to the women's locker room. Our lonely footsteps echoed against the linoleum.

"The pool closes at seven, so the first place we usually start is in the locker rooms. Make sure every locker is locked, pick up the towels, put them in these blue bins, and wheel them to the washroom. Simple enough?"

"Yeah," I answered. "Not a big deal."

"Make sure to do the men's locker room last, after closing time, for obvious reasons. Your pass will get you everywhere you need to go."

A small part of me wanted to ask her if she copied the right card. But I couldn't risk the chance of taking the card away.

"Just walkie me if you need me." She tapped the device on my hip.

"Will do," I said, shooting her a toothy grin. The door slammed behind her when she left, sending a ghostly sound reverberating through the place.

This was my chance. I waited a few moments after she left and started to cross the pool to the men's locker room. The pale underwater lights made the room glow an awkward, artificial blue. I heard a door open then slam shut. Professor Carmichael almost jumped out of his skin when he saw me standing there.

"Miss Jones!" He squealed four octaves too high, clutching his towel to his bare chest. The towel dangled above a pair of dark blue Speedo's that didn't do anything for his man parts, if you catch my drift. When he saw my expression, he covered himself, leaving his chest exposed. A small patch of taco meat that oddly resembled a head of broccoli sat between his pectorals.

"What are you doing here?" He tried to bring his voice down to a manly level, but it was too late. He had already made a fool of himself.

"I work here." I pointed to the logo on my chest. "Was there anyone else in there? I have to clean it." I crossed my arms, trying to push the image of his body out of my mind.

"I was alone." He shifted his weight on either foot. "I'll only be about twenty minutes or so." He watched me the entire time as I passed him.

"Take your time," I said, waving my card in front of the sensor. The door to the men's locker room clicked open with ease.

It was identical to the women's locker room. I didn't know what I expected to find. The red metal lockers matched the red metal benches. Dirty towels were strewn everywhere.

"Can anyone in here read?" I asked aloud, stepping over piles of towels on the floor that were just inches away from the blue bin marked 'Soiled Towels.'

I realized, earlier today, there was only one way to get Antoine out of jail. Even if I saved every paycheck I earned, it wouldn't be enough. The people at B. W. Fitz had way more money than I would ever make in a lifetime. I had to shut out the apprehensive thoughts. This was the only way. I owed it to Antoine and I owed nothing to these people.

I approached the first row of lockers and took a deep breath. "Just do it," I told myself.

I pulled the latch of the first locker. It popped open without a fight. A pair of Levi jeans was folded neatly over a pair of Ferragamo loafers. *Too bulky*, I thought, digging into one of the jeans pocket. I pulled out a Louis Vuitton wallet and out tumbled a black Movado watch.

"Carmichael," I mumbled, placing everything back where I found it and shutting the door. Too obvious. He'd know right away I stole it.

I moved on to the next row swiftly, doing the same thing, rummaging through pants pockets until I found something, anything, of value. Everything I found would be too noticeable to take. There was a man on this campus that actually walked around with a diamond encrusted Rolex on his wrist. How ridiculous was that?

I traveled to the next locker and found a wallet stuffed with cash. I wrapped my fingers around the bills when my walkie-talkie scrambled on. Selena's voice sliced through the silence.

"How's it going, Raevyn?"

My heart seized. I couldn't stop my fingers from shaking when I fumbled for the walkie-talkie. It crashed to the ground and skid across the floor. I leapt after it, slowly bringing the device towards my mouth.

"Fine," I answered, hearing my voice crack to pieces. "I'm bringing the towels up now."

"Wonderful," Selena responded.

I clipped it back on my belt loop and swiped the wad of cash in the wallet. I stuffed it in my bra and as quickly as I entered, I left.

I couldn't sleep that night. No one reported anything missing when Selena and I closed the gym, but I kept wondering when it would happen. I had about $350 stuffed in my bra when I sprinted back to my dorm after work. Someone was sure to report it missing. What if I took someone's money for rent? Or bills? Or groceries?

I couldn't allow myself to think like that. Whoever walked around with $350 in their wallet wanted someone to take the cash. I did the guy a favor. Now he knew to be more careful. Besides, he probably wouldn't even notice. More money will be pulled out of the bank account and the missing $350 will surely be forgotten because that's just what rich kids do. They didn't value anything.

Antoine needed it more. He didn't have an unlimited trust fund, or a legacy. Neither did I. I didn't owe anyone here anything.

I kept repeating that to myself while I tiptoed through the hallways toward the kitchen. My dorm was so majestic during the day, but at night, the dim lights and the ornate fixtures made it resemble a horror movie. My heartbeat quickened in my ears as I picked up the pace. I stepped into the kitchen and the light popped on overhead.

Then, the phone jangled in the next room, a loud, obnoxious tone. Fear bolted through me like lightning. If I didn't pick it up, I was sure Mrs. Potts would come running sooner or later. I dashed across the hall and into the room. It rang a third time. My brain rattled from the brash tone. I closed the accordion door behind me, hoping to diminish the sound.

"H-hello?" I twirled the cord around my finger and held my breath, but all I could hear was my heartbeat.

"Bird?" someone asked. "Is that you, Raevyn?" In the background, it sounded like cars were zooming by on the other end. I immediately recognized the voice.

"Wade?"

"I'm coming to pick up the money tomorrow." He got straight to business. Wade was always like that. I don't think I had ever seen him crack a smile. "I need you to meet me downtown."

"What time? I open at work tomorrow," I whispered into the receiver.

"Afternoon then," he suggested. "Call me on this number when you get there." He read it off to me slowly and I willed myself to memorize it despite the background noise.

"I don't know how I'll get down there," I started. "I don't have a car here." Dozens of other things whizzed through my mind, too. But I knew he didn't want to hear my excuses. Wade was cut and dry.

"You need to find a way," he demanded. "I'll be there around four and I need you to meet me downtown." I heard a set of soft footsteps approaching. "Can you do that, Bird? Can I count on you?"

"Okay," I answered, feeling my blood rise. "I'll be there. Meet me at the corner by a store called Vincent's."

He didn't even say goodbye before he hung up. I placed the receiver down softly and pulled the door back, careful not to make any noise. The kitchen light was on when I snuck out of the phone room and down the hall. I made it to the stairwell just as the light in the kitchen snapped off, blanketing the hallway in darkness once again.

Someone was there. And I knew she heard me.

Highly disappointed with their first haul, Corrine and Regina piled into Andrea's fathers' limousine immediately after me, chatting about what they planned to find down at Vincent's. The driver closed the door behind Andrea and circled around to the front. Heat enveloped us and I relaxed into the plush leather seats. Regina stripped off her Calvin Klein pea coat and fished out her cell phone.

It didn't take much convincing on my part to get them downtown for a bit of shopping. I ran into Corrine at work on the elliptical machine and told her how I felt *so* bad for missing their original shopping trip for the Mason ball. She told me that they didn't find anything they liked the first time and as soon as I planted the idea to go again she immediately texted Andrea. Before I knew it, the four of us had a shopping trip confirmed.

Once the South gate squeaked shut behind us, Andrea automatically reached for the chilled bottle of champagne. She dug her nail under the top and fog curled around her fingers as she poured herself a glass. Corrine and Regina kept talking away about what they intended to buy and what they hoped was in stock, while instinctively reaching for their own glasses. Andrea filled their glasses and then gave me an inquiring look.

"You want some or what?"

"Your dad lets you drink champagne?" I drummed my fingers along my knees and picked at the ripped fabric of my jeans. I glanced over my shoulder at the tinted partition. Could the driver see us?

"Yours doesn't?" Regina looked at me like I sprouted a third eye and told her that I came from another planet. "I keep forgetting your family is so uptight. No phone, no liquor. Are you a virgin too?" She smirked, downing the liquor all at once.

The back of my neck burned and I promptly held out my glass.

"Give me some," I demanded. Andrea filled up my glass with the bubbly liquid. She gave Regina a refill and placed the bottle back on ice.

"If you're not going to drink it"—Regina eyed me accusingly—"I'll take it."

"You don't turn down champagne," Corrine advised, taking a swig of hers. Her dark purple lipstick left a curved stain on the glass. As usual, she had on too much make-up. Under the limousine lights she could have easily been mistaken for a drag queen. I wished she knew that she was prettiest on the days where she was running late, neglecting to apply six coats of foundation.

I drank my glass down. The bitter taste hit the back of my throat and my first instinct was to spit it out. But, I swallowed instead, careful not to make a twisted face when it burned on the way down. Regina nodded approvingly and sat back in her seat.

"So who owes your father this time?" Regina crossed her legs and her foot swung happily to its own beat. Corrine's face drew into a tight line and she suddenly became so interested in her champagne flute.

"What are you talking about?" Andrea eyes slanted in Regina's direction.

"Who owes your father?" Regina repeated, opening the refrigerator that was stocked with golden champagne bottles. "You know people are always doing stuff for free for y'all." She studied her glass and continued. "You know your daddy ain't buying all this Ace of Spades." She chuckled nudging Andrea in the ribs. It was supposed to be a joke, apparently, but Andrea was not laughing.

"Whatever," she said, snatching the bottle from the bucket and refilling her glass.

"It's a joke," Regina offered. We watched as the air stiffened between the two. I looked over at Corrine who was still studying everything but the two of them. "Drea, you're not really mad, are you?" Regina asked.

"I'm straight, Reggie." She sat back in her seat and popped her ear buds in her ears.

Corrine looked over and Andrea repeated, "I'm straight."

No one said anything else for the entire ride.

I imagined Vincent's would be a huge department store. I thought I could easily get lost and disappear for a few seconds while I got the money to Wade.

I was wrong.

Vincent's was a small boutique shop with high priced items from all of the top name brands. A short, balding black man, with the loudest shirt on the face of the Earth, greeted the four of us when we walked in. I assumed he was Vincent. He quickly locked the door behind us. The store must have been closed to the public today. Andrea's father had a lot of money and even more power than she let on.

Regina, Corrine, and Andrea leaned down and gave him two air kisses. They stripped off their coats, draping them over Vincent's outstretched arm, and ventured into the racks of clothing without thinking twice.

"And who do we have here?" he asked, turning his attention to me. He didn't look me up and down. He kept his eyes locked onto mine. I, too, took off my coat.

"Raevyn Elizabeth Jones, sir." I smiled, following the girls' lead, bending down to give him two air kisses. He held his arm out and I laced my own coat over it.

"Hmm," he responded. And that was all.

He dashed into the back of the store and I followed like a lost puppy. His heeled boots clicked flamboyantly against the hardwood floor. The heels were brushed in gold, which matched his gold plated Hermés belt that unnecessarily held up his skintight black jeans.

"I pulled some pieces for you three," he said. All I could see over Regina's shoulder was the shine from his head. "I've set you up in the dressing rooms in the back. Corrine, I know how you like sequin. We just got a one-shoulder floor length dress that would look stunning on your body."

"Really? Which one?" She squealed, looking between the three closet-sized dressing room with sweeping red curtains.

"You're in the middle, honey." He chuckled. "Andrea, I've pulled some things for you in the last one and Regina, you're the one closest to the mirror. I know how you love that mirror, honey."

The three of them ran over to take a look at their options leaving Vincent and I standing in the middle of the floor.

"Are you shopping, too?" he asked, grabbing hangers off a nearby rack and sliding the coats on to them.

Regina poked her head out of the curtain. "Moral support." She quipped.

"You heard the woman," I mumbled, taking a seat on the plush ottoman in the middle of the dressing rooms. I studied my reflection in the angled mirror. A part of me felt so out of place but my father sent me here for a reason. I had to take full advantage of my opportunities at B. W. Fitz, and I wasn't talking about educationally.

"Hey, Andrea?" I cut into their excited chatter.

"What's up?" Her extensions swam gracefully around her shoulder when she peeked out of the curtain. Her mood had changed drastically from then minutes ago. Shopping could do that to a girl with no limit on her credit card.

"I think I left something in the limo."

"Garrison should still be out there," she answered. "I'll call him and see if he can find it. What is *it* exactly?" Her thumb hovered over the screen of her phone.

"I'll just go get it. No biggie." I jumped up.

She shrugged. "Suit yourself."

The wind blasted my cheeks while I ventured up the sidewalk looking for Wade. Once I reached the corner, a pair of hands accosted me and pulled me into the alley. Before I could scream out I heard a familiar voice.

"Damn, Bird. I almost didn't recognize you looking like Little Miss Hollywood." Wade pulled me in for a long hug. "Antoine told me to give you that." He stepped back, admiring me as if he was taking a mental picture.

His brown eyes were mysterious. Wade was always nice to me, but at first glance, he was threatening, bundled up in a bubble coat with an Armani Exchange printed hat pulled down over his ears. The toes of his Timberland boots were wet with snow. I could tell he'd gotten bigger, stronger even, from the last time I saw him.

"How is he?" I asked, digging around in my purse for the money. I knew he'd want to get this over with quickly. And I needed to get back inside Vincent's before anyone noticed I wasn't at the limo.

"He's hanging in there. He's strong," he replied. I noticed the scar on his face where he was cut in a really bad fight. If Antoine wasn't there to push the guy, the blade would have blinded Wade for sure. Like me, Wade was indebted to Antoine, and that's why I pushed the guilty thoughts out of my mind when I handed him the money. He quickly stuffed it in his pocket.

"That's five hundred," I reported. I managed to nick a few extra hundreds from a wallet in the women's locker room before I left work today.

"Cool," he answered, pulling me in for another hug. "I'm getting out of here. Stay smart, Bird. Don't let these rich kids get to your head."

"'Course not," I assured him.

"Aight," he responded, looking me up and down. His eyebrow rose in doubt.

"These are only clothes," I pointed out. "I'm still the same."

He kissed my cheek softly. "Take care of yourself, Bird." He took off across the street and jumped into a midnight black Dodge Charger and zoomed away. I high-tailed it back to Vincent's, hoping no one would notice how long I'd been gone.

When I walked back inside, everyone was fawning over Andrea in a floor-length red dress. It was backless with angled cutouts on the sides, leaving her amazing mid-section exposed. It was elegant yet edgy, perfect for a ball and perfect for Andrea.

"You have to get that," Corrine said giddily. She caught my reflection in the mirror. "Come on, don't you think she looks amazing, Rae?"

Everyone turned around. Andrea flipped her hair into a messy bun and posed with her long, lanky fingers gripping her hip.

"Stunning," I confirmed.

Andrea stepped off of the platform. "Then I'll get it."

Corrine squealed with delight. Her sequin gown sparkled as she hopped up and down. Vincent was right; the dress was made for her. I looked around for Regina. I realized she wasn't out here rejoicing with the bunch.

"Reggie," I called. "What did you choose?"

"She has something special." Vincent bounced happily out of the room.

"Well, let us see!" Corrine squealed again. She could be annoying at times, but she was genuinely happy for everyone and I appreciated that about her. That quality was hard to find in most people.

Regina slowly pulled her curtain back and my mouth could have scraped the floor. She stepped onto the platform and an audible gasp resounded around the room. There were no words to describe how regal Regina looked in the backless white peplum pencil dress. The exaggerated peplum accentuated her hips, and the back of the gown sloped to a V. It stopped just after her waistline to make it sexy but it didn't travel past that, making it classy. I spotted a line of ink above her hips. Regina had a tattoo?

"If you don't get that, I will," I teased.

"Oh, this is coming home with momma," she said, smoothing her hands down the sides of her hips. She straightened her back gracefully. Everything about Regina screamed perfection.

Vincent came back inside with four glasses of bubbling champagne on a silver platter. Regina, Corrine, and Andrea ran up, each taking a glass. After an imploring pause, Vincent pushed the lone glass towards me and I took it. I would have to get used to all of the free alcohol.

"Congratulations to my favorite girls," he shouted at the top of his lungs. "Y'all are going to kill it at the Mason ball!" We all took a swig of the champagne. That time, it went down easier.

A beat later, we were back in the limo, laughing until we cried on the way back to school. I wanted to bottle those moments when it wasn't about clothes or money. We were just four friends having a good time together. At that very moment, for the first time, I felt like an equal. Today was a good day.

The semester was coming to a close so everyone was scrambling. People moved in waves from the dorms to the library, the caf, and the gym. Days became shorter and the workload was getting heavier. Based on the way my grades were shaping up, it would take a miracle to even get a 3.0 at the end of the semester, let alone a 3.5, and Miss Tanner was not going to let me forget it.

She showed up a few minutes before Professor Carmichael's class, bundled up in a coat that was two sizes too big for her fragile body. If I looked close enough, I was certain that I saw her shivering.

"Miss Jones." She smiled. Her teeth were too big for her mouth, Hillary Duff style.

"What do you want?" I snapped, coming to a stop right outside of Carmichael's door.

Like clockwork, he poked his head out. "Miss Jones, you have two minutes to get inside."

"Randy," Miss Tanner said light-heartedly at his presence. He looked over at her and a cunning smile passed over his lips for a while. It suddenly disappeared when the two of them realized I was still standing there, witnessing their weird—and uncomfortable, I might add—interaction.

He cleared his throat. "Sylvia. Nice to see you."

"Likewise," she replied. "I was just telling your student here that she was cutting it dangerously close with her pre-honors GPA." She smirked.

He was Randy? "And I was just telling your colleague that I still have time to pull my grades up."

"Not much time," Carmichael interjected.

I turned on the spot and proceeded inside the classroom.

"Just a few more weeks, Miss Jones," she called after me with the voice that made my stomach turn. I knew the two of them would make sure I didn't spend another semester here longer than I was supposed to.

I stayed up late to finish my Poly-Sci paper just to wake up at the crack of dawn to open at the gym. I was knee-deep in an Aframhis paper when Dre waltzed into the gym Saturday morning. It had been a few weeks since I saw him outside of French class. We both didn't have time to talk much. I cradled my head in my hands just as the automatic doors slid open. I didn't look up, thinking it would be another student coming in to blow off steam before pulling an all-nighter in the library.

"Sleeping on the job, huh?" I knew it was Dre from his southern twang. I couldn't hold back the smile that crept across my face.

"Just resting my eyes," I joked, holding my hand out for his key pass. I swiped his card and his face popped up on my computer screen. "There ya go." I handed his card back.

He grabbed a towel from the bin beside me and slung it over his shoulder. "What time do you get off?"

"Noon," I answered, suppressing a yawn. "I have an Aframhis paper to finish and my Mass Comm homework from last week." I had a whole list of assignments I had to get through, but I didn't want Dre thinking I was a total slacker.

The truth was, I'd been working so much to try and save money, that I'd been neglecting my homework. The bright side was I had almost $1,000 to give to Wade this time. I managed to snag a pair of Chanel earrings from the drain in the swimming pool. Who swims in earrings? Chanel earrings at that. These people were making it too easy.

Dre cut into my thoughts. "Can I join you?"

"At the admin desk?" I blurted.

"At the library." He laughed, shaking his head at me. "You are going there, right?" He leaned on the counter, his arm only inches from mine. I leaned back on my stool, not knowing what to do with my hands. I wished I had more experience in the boy department. Antoine was my only boyfriend. He was the only one I ever loved and the only one I ever trusted. It was downright weird to have guys like Dre fawn over me. I didn't know what to say or do half the time. Dre seemed to pick up on that immediately. "I, uh, have a bunch of work to finish up, too," he explained. "Do you...mind if I join you?"

"Not at all," I answered, failing miserably at hiding my blushing cheeks.

He smiled. "Cool. I'll meet you around two?"

"See you then." I tried not to stare while he walked away.

Something told me that Dre was caught up on all of his work.

I made sure to load up on power food before meeting Dre at the library. I moved through the cafeteria without interruption. There weren't many people, which made it easy to spot Jeffrey sitting at our usual table, alone. I headed over to the a la carte tray and grabbed a couple bottles of water, some fruit, and a small salad. My hand hovered over a triple chocolate brownie, but I decided against it. Regina would disapprove. I headed over to our table and sat down beside Jeffrey.

"What's up?" he asked, looking up from his math homework. Confusing equations lined the pages. Eraser marks, where he'd made mistakes over and over, left the notebook paper a murky gray. He flipped his pencil between his fingers and caressed his lined forehead.

"Loading up on food before I head to the library to finish the paper for Carmichael."

Jeffrey shook his head. "I just finished. It was brutal." He erased heavily again, brushing pieces of pink eraser into the seat of his navy blue Dockers. They were cuffed at the ankle, revealing his bright orange socks, which matched the orange stitching in his wrinkled Polo T-shirt.

He looked exhausted and there was no bow tie. Usually he was well pressed and groomed like a GQ model. I knew something was wrong.

"Sounds like you could use a break," I offered. Just then, I spotted Dre walking into the cafeteria. He met a few people on the opposite end of the room. I knew it was only a matter of time before he saw me with Jeffrey. My stomach stirred.

"What are those?" He laughed, rubbing his tired red eyes. "I have to make honors next year. I don't *do* breaks."

"Need that yellow blazer, huh?" I asked, discreetly stealing a look at Dre who was engaged in conversation with a short, light skinned girl. She laughed obnoxiously loud and swatted at his chest. Dre playfully doubled over from the blow. Who was *she?*

"Absolutely," Jeff answered. "Everyone in my family graduated with a white blazer. I refuse to be the only one who doesn't. That yellow blazer is the first step." He let out an enormous yawn, stretching his muscular arms behind his head. "Gotta keep going." He rubbed his hands over his face where scratchy stubble began to grow in.

I took a long look at him. "How long have you been up?"

"Nineteen, maybe twenty hours," he guessed, shrugging his shoulders like it was no big deal.

My eyes felt like they would pop out of their sockets. "Are you serious?"

"I gotta do what I gotta do." He shrugged again.

I knew there was more than he was letting on, but I decided not to press the issue right then. He obviously had a lot on his plate. I didn't want to be the one to scold him for being an overachiever. Plus, I noticed that Dre had spotted me and was heading my way. I felt my face get hot in anticipation.

"Are you headed to the library now?" Jeffrey asked. "I'll join you." He started to pack up his books, tossing them inside his messenger bag and I thought I heard something rattle around. I knew that sound from anywhere but before I could question him, or my sanity, Dre approached the table like clockwork.

"It's almost two, mademoiselle." Dre pointed at his Cartier watch. He held his hand out, waiting patiently for me to place mine in his. Jeffrey's brow furrowed at the stranger. He looked between Dre and me slowly, and I couldn't tell what was running through his head.

My heart felt like it was running a marathon. "Dre." I coughed into my fist, ignoring his outstretched hand. "This is Jeffrey." I nodded toward Jeffrey who was now turned around in his seat, acknowledging Dre's presence. Jeffrey was downright staring at Dre as if he knew him from somewhere.

"Andre Pierre Mouton from New Orleans, Louisiana," Dre introduced himself and immediately shook hands with Jeffrey.

Jeffrey squinted as if he was trying to see Dre at a different angle. "Jeffrey Vincent Eugene Donnelly the fourth of Donnelly, Brandt, and Associates in Manhattan, New York."

I wanted to disappear. I wanted to melt into the table. "You two going to the library?" Jeffrey asked with an accusatory tone.

"At two," I answered, careful not to look at his face.

"It's 2:02," Dre volunteered. "We are now late." He laughed, dodging the daggers Jeffrey's eyes were throwing. "Are you ready?"

I glanced at Jeffrey who pretended as if he was poring over his math homework again. He didn't even look my way. "See you, Jeff." I brushed his shoulder. He shrugged me off.

"What's the deal with your boyfriend?" Dre whispered as we began to walk away from the table.

"He's not my boyfriend," I answered.

"You sure about that?" Dre inquired, holding the door open for me. The wind chilled me to the core. I realized that I wasn't so sure anymore.

Between the altercation with Jeffrey and Dre's incessant flirting, it was safe to say I didn't get any work done in the library. Nearly four hours passed and I only managed to get about a half-page typed for Carmichael's paper.

Every five seconds, it seemed, Dre would reach over and tickle me or 'accidentally' brush his pinky against mine. It was cute at first, but now it was downright annoying.

After I showed him for the thirtieth time how to format an annotated bibliography, I said, "I, um, really have to get this done." I gestured to the document open on my laptop. The waiting cursor blinked at me impatiently on the blank page. Nothing was coming to me. I could barely concentrate.

He scooted his chair closer, which I didn't think could be anatomically possible.

"Let me see what you're working on." He pulled the screen towards him and his eyes traveled slowly over the little I'd typed. "Maybe I can help."

"It's part of the final for Carmichael," I explained and pulled the exam paper from my bag. "We have to identify the problems, if any, in the Black elite community."

"If any?" Dre echoed, taking the paper from me and reading over the directions himself. "Thank God I don't have to deal with this class. I would fail miserably."

"Why do you say that?"

"There's a million things wrong with it." He chuckled, knitting his fingers behind his neck and leaning back in his chair. Two of the pegs lifted off the ground while he continued, "You think he wants to hear that though? From what I hear about this Carmichael guy, he seems to love his privileged lifestyle."

I remembered he was a non-legacy. Of course he considered the legacies to be privileged. But, he wasn't too far off. I knew he wasn't paying for the expensive clothing and watches by himself. Just because he was a non-legacy didn't mean that he wasn't rich. Everyone here that hadn't done an honest days work or hadn't gone to bed hungry was privileged to me but I knew most of them didn't see it that way.

"If you want to pass, you should write what you know he wants to hear."

I pulled the laptop back toward me and totally ditched my original plan of agreeing with Carmichael's views. There were tons of problems with these rich people and I wanted Carmichael to know each one, starting with the ridiculous idea of legacies.

After about twenty minutes I had almost two single-spaced pages of content. My fingers were tapping ferociously against the keyboard. I realized that it was becoming less of an academic assignment and more of a rant. The thought jumped in my mind to backspace the whole thing and start over. I did need to pass Carmichael's class to stay a student here, but I couldn't let an opportunity like this slip away.

Dre leaned over when I flexed my cramped fingers. "You stopped."

"I think I'm finished."

His eyes ran over my screen. "Aren't…you a legacy?" He read more and his lips curled into a curious smile.

I whipped the laptop in my direction. "Yeah," I said. My face was beginning to get hot. "But I do have my own opinion about things."

"That's weird," he acknowledged. "Most legacies take so much pride in it." He placed his hand over his heart. "My father is such-and-such," he mimicked in a girly voice. He flipped his dreadlocks dramatically over his shoulder like I'd seen Andrea do with her extensions. "My mother can do this and that." He pushed his hand in my face. "I don't eat real meals. Are those potatoes? Nu-unnh, just almonds thank you very much." He snapped his fingers in a circle, pursing his lips and cocking his head to the side.

"You're pretty good at that," I said, clutching my sides; tears were streaming down my eyes from laughing so hard.

"Seriously." He caught his breath from laughter. "You're the first legacy I've met who hates their legacy."

"I don't hate it." I twirled a lock of hair around my finger thinking of the right words to say. "I think we all should be able to create our own destinies." Dre nodded, agreeing. "For example, just because my father is a mortician doesn't mean I enjoy embalming old people. What if I want to be…" I trailed, realizing at that moment I never really had an idea of what I wanted to be. It hit me like a punch to the gut. All I'd ever concentrated on was being with Antoine. He was my whole world.

But, at B. W. Fitz, I had choices. I had opportunities. I had a future here. What did I want to *be*? Who did I want to be?

Jeffrey had his future aligned for him since before he was born. I wished he knew that he could be whomever he wanted, too. He didn't have to get that stupid yellow blazer if he didn't want to. But something told me that no matter what I said, no matter how late he had to stay up, or how much he had to study, he would get that blazer.

"A singer," Dre guessed, finishing my sentence, snapping me back to the present moment.

"Uh, right." I slid my clammy palms on the thighs of my jeans. "What if I wanted to be a singer? Why should I have to ditch my personal dreams to preserve my legacy?"

Dre shrugged. "I heard that's just the way it goes."

"Unfortunately." I turned back to my work. I couldn't imagine the pressure of being suffocated by my parent's career. That wasn't living at all. "Be glad *you* can choose."

Dre's lips flattened into a straight line. "Right."

When I arrived at my dorm I noticed someone sitting on the front steps. He or she was hunched over, in a thin cardigan, shivering. If it was Miss Tanner I was going to flip. I got closer and realized the shadowy lean figure was Jeffrey.

"What are you doing out here?" I ran over to him. "It's freezing. Why didn't you go inside?"

His head lifted up slowly as if it was too heavy for his neck to hold. It took too long for his glossed-over eyes to focus on mine. He seemed to be totally out of it.

"Jeffrey!" I gripped his shoulders. He placed his frigid hands on top of mine.

"I'm fine." It was only two words but they seemed to roll slowly like molasses off his tongue. "I've been waiting out here for you." I let my hands drop lifelessly by my side. He was delirious. Or he was…my mind backtracked to hours ago in the cafeteria. There was that rattling…in his bag. I knew that sound. But, it couldn't be. *No, Raevyn. You're tripping*, I thought.

"You what?" I crept closer, trying to catch a glimpse of his eyes again to make sure I wasn't seeing what I thought I was. Was Jeffrey…high?

He slipped his messenger bag off his shoulder and dug around in the front pocket. He pulled out a small square of cardstock. It rustled in his naked hand.

"I got it." He smiled up at me goofily.

"Got what?" I asked, taking the paper from him. I pulled the card out of the envelope and let my eyes scan over the words that were written in beautiful calligraphy.

"Is this?" My heart tumbled over with confused emotions. I resisted the urge to jump up and down.

"Your plus one," Jeffrey confirmed. "Wanna be my date?"

"Me? Jeffrey, I don't have a dress or shoes. I would have to press my hair and that could take hours," I rambled, thinking of all the things that I would have to do to prepare for the Mason ball. If it was as exclusive as Regina made it seem, I was going to be so out of place. God, what would I wear? How long had it been since I wore heels? Prom?

He stood up abruptly, towering over me. Instinctively, I backed up, bumping against the railing. He closed the space that slipped between our bodies and placed his icy, calloused hand around the back of my neck, pulling me close. His embrace sent a chill down my spine. My legs shook like pudding and I couldn't stop myself from falling into him.

"Will you go with me?" he asked, only inches away. His sweet breath warmed my face and the invitation fluttered out of my hand.

Right then, the whole world seemed to stop.

My mind drew a blank. I couldn't think of any words, so I nodded.

Before I knew it, his lips brushed mine, gently at first, almost as if it were a mistake. Somewhere, in the pit of my belly a butterfly bat its wings. He grabbed me closer, gripping my small frame against his solid chest. I allowed his tongue to swipe playfully at mine. His lips devoured mine and I willingly submitting to his demands for more.

I lost track of everything. I wanted to stay there, in his arms, consuming each other until time stopped and started again. I wanted to bottle this moment and keep it close to my heart.

My purse slid off my shoulder and crashed to the ground. The sound snapped both of us back to reality. He shot backwards, away from me. My lips were buzzing, still drunk on his passion.

"What just happened?" He laughed, wiping his mouth.

"I don't know," I answered, picking up my purse and the invitation that started this whole thing. "I don't know," I repeated. My head was swimming. I hoped he couldn't feel the burning heat I emitted. Or the way my body yearned for his presence.

"Listen." Jeffrey looked over at me with flushed cheeks. I couldn't meet his gaze. He dug into his pocket and pulled out his wallet. He flipped it open and pondered over a slew of cards before holding one out. "Get yourself a dress, some shoes, and all that other shit you said you needed."

"I'm not taking that!" I slapped his hand away.

"Please, let me do this for you."

"I'm not taking your money." Was I everyone's charity case? Did they all know I couldn't afford to go here? Was it that obvious? Was he in on the scheme with Regina to get me out of here?

"Raevyn, stop." Jeffrey's voice was exhausted. "I know there are a million things running through that mind of yours." He tapped my temple. "Let me do this for you, please. I want to."

I eyed him for a while before he felt comfortable enough to slip the card in the front pocket of my jeans. He took that opportunity to hook his finger in my belt loop and pulled me close. He planted a soft kiss on my forehead, then another on my nose, then my lips. I made a point to breathe in his scent.

Clean, fresh, musky, sweet. That was Jeffrey.

"Jeffrey?" I whispered with my face buried in his neck. His skin against my skin. My heart drumming along to the same beat of his.

"Don't question it." He pulled away from me and the world began spinning on its correct axis again. The cold returned. My erratic thoughts returned.

He pulled his bag back on his shoulder, taking one last look at me. His eyes were bloodshot and barely open. He didn't smell like weed. So maybe he wasn't high. I decided to blame it on his deliriousness. But why was my gut telling me that it was something else?

"Get some sleep," I said to him before I turned to go inside. "You look like shit."

Sunday morning Andrea and I went to service. It was never mandatory in my house that we attended church. Sunday morning was just pre-Monday, as my dad always said. But here, it seemed like much more of a requirement. Every single Sunday everyone got dressed, and I do mean dressed, for the 8 a.m. service.

Regina and Corrine were in the choir and today was Corrine's big solo. She had been waiting on this solo for a while and once the lead soprano got mysteriously sick last weekend, Corrine jumped at the chance to sing.

We sat in our usual spots like we did during the morning announcements. The heat was pumping. It almost felt like a sauna. Andrea peeled off her coat once we sat down, revealing a tight, black wrap dress. It cinched her waist, making her behind poke out. There was no way anyone in the sanctuary could miss it. I tried to keep my eyes away during praise and worship.

Before long, Jeffrey bolted into the sanctuary, and I felt my heart do a back flip. All last night I relived our kiss. I thought I was dreaming, but I really kissed Jeffrey. And he really kissed me back. I sat up in bed at 6 a.m. thinking about the perfect outfit to wear when I saw him. What should I do? Act like nothing happened? Would we hold hands? Were we together now?

I tried not to look too excited, expecting him to take the open seat next to me as usual. But, for some reason he sat a couple rows back and my mind raced in different directions. Was it because of yesterday? Did I do something wrong?

As soon as I took a good look at him, my hopes of our whimsical romance deflated, shriveling into a wad of nothingness. He looked more disheveled than he had the day before. Andrea tapped her Kate Spade watch and shot him a 'what the hell is wrong with you?' look, as well as about three hundred other students. He didn't even look up. She whipped around, facing me accusingly, and I shrugged my shoulders.

Everyone must have had the same thoughts. Jeffrey was never late and he was never seen out without looking dapper. In the dark yesterday I couldn't make out how scruffy his beard was or how much his hair had grown out. Something was *very* wrong with him. And maybe, just maybe my gut was right.

Corrine sang beautifully and angelically, but no one was focused on her voice, which was unfortunate. She looked so happy while she was singing, like she was a 5-year-old at her first tap recital and we were her proud parents. I tried my best to pay attention but my mind was only running wild with thoughts of Jeffrey.

From the sanctuary, I could see Regina's hands moving swiftly under her robe. She must have been texting Andrea. I managed to find Brandon in the crowd and he had the same puzzled look.

Jeffrey was fidgeting the whole service. His leg bobbed up and down or he picked at his fingers. I glanced back at him and he was staring blankly, unseeingly at his hands. Jeffrey must have felt our glares the entire service because once the benediction was delivered he bolted toward the door. No one had a chance to talk to him.

I tried to convince myself that I was seeing things but I knew those symptoms from anywhere. The rattling sound resounded in my brain. He reminded me of my mom when she came down from a binge and I felt like I was about to throw up.

⋆⟶⟵⋆

Corrine caught up to the three of us in the cafeteria. She didn't even bother asking what we thought of her solo because she knew by now what everyone was talking about, and it wasn't her perfect singing voice.

"Has anyone talked to him?" She bit into a forkful of her vegetable omelette.

"He won't answer the phone," Regina reported dejectedly. "Did you see his face? He looked like he hasn't shaved in weeks. He looked—"

"It's probably just stress," I cut in. "He is bugging out about finals."

"Everyone bugs out about finals," Andrea snapped. "No reason to walk around looking like a damn vagabond." She turned her nose up, flicking her hair over her shoulder. She reached over me and dug her fork into the steamy middle of Corrine's omelette.

Annoyed, Corrine pushed her plate towards her. "Here, have some."

"How sweet of you." Andrea batted her false eyelashes.

"How do you know?" Regina asked accusingly. Her eyes, like darts, shot through me.

"Know what?" I responded, occupying the awkward moment by digging around in Corrine's omelette too. I heard her let out a clipped sigh.

"How do you know that Jeffrey is bugging about finals? Have you talked to him?" She tried, and failed, to take the edge off her voice. What was it about Jeffrey that Regina felt she had to defend all the time?

"Last night," I admitted. I dug into my Prada tote bag. "He gave me this." I showed them my invitation to the Mason ball. Only Corrine gasped, as usual. Andrea and Regina exchanged quick curious glances and I acted like I didn't notice.

"Looks like you need to make another call to Vincent." Regina pointed out.

Andrea smirked. I knew it was her attempt at being polite. She pulled out her cell phone, dialed a number, and walked away from the table.

After that, the rest of us ate in silence.

The week zoomed by and when I arrived to French class on Friday, Dre was sitting on the opposite side of the room. He was busy writing, with his right hand, and didn't look up when I walked in. Professor Bonhomme must have moved his seat because of our antics.

A square package wrapped in soft blue tissue paper and topped with a loopy gold bow was waiting for me at my seat. It didn't take me long to figure out who placed it there. I looked over at Dre and his eyes met mine hungrily.

"Open it," he mouthed. A smile crept slowly across his face. "Hurry," he urged, shooing his hands at me. It was sweet to see how excited he was.

Inside was a brand new iPhone. I picked it up in disbelief. It was so small and lightweight that it felt like a toy. This was definitely an upgrade from the bulky Samsung I used to own. Behind the phone was a pocket-sized 'French for Dummies' book. The phone vibrated with a text message from Dre: **So u won't have to cheat anymore.**

My heart fluttered with delight. Dre was certainly my Antoine away from Antoine.

I typed to him: **Thank you.**

My phone buzzed a second later with: **You're very welcome, mademoiselle.**

―――――――――――――――――――――

Dre caught up with me after class. I wasn't watching where I was going. I was too busy playing with my new phone. I almost slammed into a light pole when Dre caught me by the arm.

"I see you're enjoying that."

"Yeah." I blushed, side-stepping the pole that would have been in a nasty head-on collision with my cranium. "I can see why Regina is always on it."

"They're addicting but definitely not worth messing up that beautiful face." He trailed his finger along my cheek and I dipped away from his gesture.

"Too much?" He asked as if he was going through a checklist in his mind.

"I'm just..." I started to speak but I wanted to get the words right. "I'm just not used to this." The lightweight phone suddenly felt like it weighed fifteen pounds.

"Having a cell phone?"

"No." I exhaled, trying to silence the dozens of thoughts running at top speed through my mind. I sifted through them all quickly attempting to find the perfect explanation. "Guys don't normally do things like this for me where I'm from."

"Right, no guys on Venus," Dre joked, smiling down at me.

"I-I..." I stuttered. "You don't even know me."

Dre slammed to a stop. "Raevyn, I don't want anything from you, if that's what you're thinking." The playfulness was gone out of his voice. His deep russet eyes grabbed mine. "I just wanted to do something nice for you and that's all."

"I don't know what to say," I admitted, thinking back to the other night with Jeffrey. It seemed like every guy here wanted to take care of me. But, why? I was no beauty queen like Andrea. I was just a regular girl who would rather wear Faded Glory sweatpants before I paid hundreds of dollars to have some brand name screen printed on my butt. I wasn't rich and if it weren't for Regina, the most expensive item of clothing I owned would've been my Barney sweater.

"All you have to say is thank you." He paused. "You're different, Raevyn. I noticed that the first day I met you."

My palms dampened and it wasn't because of my gloves. Did he *know*?

"How do you mean?"

"For one"—he chuckled—"I've never met a legacy who didn't want to be in a legacy."

"I never said—"

Dre held his hand up. "I know what you said but most legacies are so stuck up and pompous. You couldn't care less about those things. You're different, Rae. It's like you understand what I've been trying to explain to my parents all along." He exhaled as if he'd been holding that in for a long time.

"I'm very proud of my legacy, Dre," I prefaced. "I just think we should be able to choose. We shouldn't have to be forced."

"Exactly!" Dre's eyes lit up. "That's what makes you different," he exclaimed. My feet fumbled over one another when he abruptly pulled me close to him. "I know we don't know each other that well, but, I want to get to know you better. I want you to know that you can trust me."

Immediately my throat closed. Everything seemed to shut down in my body. I couldn't breathe and I couldn't think. I couldn't do anything but stand there, numb. I wanted to say something, anything that could get me out of this, but for once, there was nothing conjuring in my mind.

After awkward silence gnawed away at the moment he pleaded, "Say something."

"Okay." The words scratched my throat on the way up. My mind was so frazzled that was all I could manage to get out.

I skipped French class not only because I wanted to avoid Dre, but because Friday was the only day Andrea's father could his driver, Garrison, to take us to Vincent's.

"It's either at five," she said to me with an attitude, "or not at all."

"Five is fine," I answered, making a U-turn in the middle of campus and heading back toward my dorm. Since I didn't have to make the journey to the foreign language building, I could snag a little something from the gym for Antoine.

"Cool." Andrea didn't say anything else before ending the conversation.

The gym was practically empty when I went inside. Selena sat alone at the reception desk, doodling on a pad next to her.

"Oh hey, doll." Her eyes brightened when she saw me. She stood up and hugged me over the desk. Selena hugged me every single time she saw me as if I would disappear. "Your girls are upstairs." She pointed to the roof.

"My girls?"

"Regina and um"—she snapped her fingers—"the little light skinned one with the cute freckles."

"Corrine."

"Yep. She rented out the studio. I usually charge Regina by the hour but there was no one here. I let her have it."

"Oh," I responded, taking off in the direction of the studios upstairs.

"Raevyn?" Selena called just before I reached the stairs. When I turned around she asked, "Have you been getting any reports of suspicious behavior lately?"

My heart fell to my feet. "Suspicious behavior?" I repeated as if the words were foreign.

"Yeah," Selena said. "People have been reporting stolen goods."

I cupped my hand over my mouth. "Exactly." Selena bought the act. "Some say it's money, others say it's their watch or their cufflinks. It's never happened before," she finished airily.

"If I hear or see anything, I'll let you know." I had to get out of there pronto.

"Thanks! See ya, doll!" Selena called after me as I dashed upstairs toward the studios.

On the top floor I could hear the faint sounds of soft music floating in the air from the mirror-lined studio where hot yoga usually took place.

I crept closer to the door and spotted Corrine on the floor, clutching her iPod.

"Again?" She looked up apprehensively at Regina who was dripping with sweat. She was hunched over, her hands braced on her knees. Her back heaved in and out.

"Again," Regina demanded.

"Maybe you should take a break," Corrine offered. She held a bottle of water out to Regina who refused. "We've been at it all night. I don't think you can get any better in ten minutes."

"Run...it...again."

Corrine popped on the music without hesitation and Regina maneuvered around the floor angelically as if she wasn't dog tired just a few seconds ago. That explained why Regina was so graceful, so poised. Regina was...a dancer?

I stood idle and watched Regina. She was magical. When the music ended Corrine asked, "Are you satisfied now?"

"No," Regina sputtered. "Didn't you see me stumble? I'll never make it into the program like that."

"Are you sure you even want to go through with this?" Corrine handed her the bottle of water. Regina sucked it down. "Your dad is going to flip his shit if he finds out you're dancing again."

"That's the thing." Regina slipped her body into her coat and Corrine did the same. She unplugged her iPod from the wall and Regina let her hair down from the ballerina bun atop her head. "He won't ever find out."

The whole world around me moved in slow motion.

The clock on the dash read 6:37 p.m., just before the seatbelt grabbed my throat. I heard Antoine scream for me, his hands flew frantically, trying to gain control of the car, but it was too late. The cash rained around us, catapulting this way and that, blocking his view of the road. The steering wheel jerked demonically like someone else was driving.

We fishtailed then whipped in the opposite direction. Chunks of gravel jumped, popping against the windshield.

Antoine stomped on the brake. Our tires skid across the road, smoke billowed in the air, and then it felt like we were flying.

My stomach rose then dropped, and before I could scream, before I realized what was happening, my mouth collided with the dashboard when the car finally slammed to a stop.

Steam rolled like black clouds and the world just would not. stop. ringing. What the fuck was that ringing? The metallic taste of blood mixed with the overwhelming smell of burned rubber made me nauseated. A white-hot pain shot through my neck and my brain throbbed so violently that I knew it would explode at any second.

The foggy scenery floated into view. I was in an accident. A car accident. Antoine. I was with Antoine. I was alive. Was he alive?

"Pooh," I managed to say. His name lodged in my throat. I couldn't breathe. I reached carefully for the snap that latched the seatbelt onto my *neck. I pressed the button and the belt whipped past my face, securing itself back into place.*

My fingers found the stitching in the seat beside me, but there was no Antoine. I blinked through the haziness, feeling the milky smoke coat my throat. I wanted to get up. I had to see Antoine, but my legs were pinned under the mangled front end of the car.

"Pooh," I cried again but only silence answered back.

"Antoine!" A scream escaped.

"Antoine!" My throat burned when I bolted up. My eyes adjusted to the darkness and as the haze of my dreams wore off, I recognized my surroundings. I was in bed at B. W. Fitz.

"You're home." I pinched myself. "You're home."

My heartbeat calmed and then Regina flung my door open, barreling inside.

"What's going on?" She ran over to me, placing her cool hand to my forehead. I guessed she thought I had a fever because I was sweating like a whore in church.

"Bad dream," I reassured her, swatting her hands away. "I'm fine." I wished I could forget that day even happened.

"You want to talk about it?" Regina took a seat on the edge of my bed. I could barely make out her face, shadowed by the night, but I could hear the concern in her voice.

"It's just a dream."

"Sounded like more than a dream to me," she mumbled. "Who is Antoine?"

"What?" I wanted to kick myself.

"You were screaming at the top of your lungs. I thought someone was in here."

I chuckled, grateful for the segue. "What were you going to do if someone was? You didn't even have a weapon."

"I'll have you know"—she crossed the room, making sure I took in her slim frame—"I have my black belt. I could have karate chopped him or something." Her comment made me remember seeing her in the dance studio almost a week ago. I wondered if she got into whatever program she was applying to.

"Thanks, Reggie," I said. "But I'll be fine." I slid off my bed and tiptoed over to my dresser. I unbuttoned my pajamas that were damp with sweat and changed into a fresh pair.

"Get some rest," she advised. "Tomorrow's the big day!"

"See you in the morning," I said before she quietly pulled my door closed.

It took a couple of hours to fall asleep again partly because I was worried about everything under the sun. Regina flip-flopped between being a bitch and being concerned for me so much that I didn't know what to believe. The only person I knew that could possibly be a true friend was Corrine because she kept her emotions on her sleeve. But Regina and Andrea were questionable at best. Did they know I wasn't really a legacy? Had they known all along? And what about that conversation in the booth in the middle of the night? Were they still conspiring against me? I realized I hadn't had a chance to tell Jeffrey about my thoughts. But, given his mental state, could I trust him with anything?

Butterflies stirred wildly in my stomach when my mind flashed back to the other night when he and I kissed. My heartbeat was calm and steady and my mind was completely blank. I wasn't worried about my grades, my friendships, or money. The only thing that mattered then was Jeffrey and me.

I wished I could go back to that perfect night because everything around me was starting to change. What I thought would be easy was way harder than I expected. B. W. Fitz was so different from home. The things that seemed normal at home were the very things that were bringing so much attention to me here.

Dre, who insisted on courting me endlessly, was confusing my heart even more. Jeffrey was amazing—full of confidence and sociable; however, Dre was the total opposite. He was very casual, laid-back, and collected. He didn't have to be the center of attention and he felt familiar. He felt like Antoine.

But wasn't I supposed to be staying away from Antoine? Instead, I was jumping at every open shift to work at the gym to pilfer more money and potentially get caught in the act. I was making every excuse to get downtown to drop the money to Wade.

I was supposed to be blending in at Fitz. What was happening to me? It felt like my soul, my loyalty, was being torn in two different directions. Keeping the two worlds separate was harder than I expected.

I glanced at my bedside clock. The red numbers stared back at me. 4 a.m. Regina was right, I needed rest because tomorrow I was going to be one of the 'it' girls. I was going to be pampered and styled like a legacy. For once, I was excited about something at B. W. Fitz.

Andrea had us on a strict schedule. We'd wake up early and have brunch downtown, then get massages, manicures, and pedicures. Corrine insisted that we all get waxed but I steered very clear from that subject. I couldn't imagine being spread eagle on a table for a stranger, well, for anyone actually.

I willed myself to shut my mind down because I knew tomorrow would be epic.

Seven a.m. arrived quicker than my body expected. Andrea almost kicked my door down when she found out I had fallen back asleep after her first wake up call. I pulled on a pair of Juicy Couture sweatpants and stuffed my feet into Uggs. I struggled to the bathroom and brushed my teeth and hair to the best of my ability and met the three of them in the living room.

"Who pissed in your Cheerios?" Andrea lifted up her sunglasses, taking a long look at me. "You look like hell."

Regina held her hand up in protest. "Our princess had a rough night."

"What happened?" Corrine asked. Her green eyes grew wide with concern. "Is everything okay?"

"I'm fine," I answered. I pulled my dress and my bag off the couch. "Are we ready to go?"

"No," Andrea started. "We've just been standing here waiting—"

"Quit it," Regina scolded and Andrea shut her mouth immediately, not before giving her a look that could easily slice her skin off.

She threw her shoulders back. "Limo's downstairs. Garrison isn't going to wait forever," Andrea said to the three of us while heading out of the door. We all gathered our belongings and followed.

Corrine touched my arm softly. "We can talk about it later," she assured me. "After the ball?"

"I'm fine, really." My heart softened at Corrine's concern. As much as I wanted to let her in on the things that had been bothering me lately, I knew I couldn't.

We all loaded into the elevator without saying a word, that is, until we met Mrs. Potts on the ground floor. Her presence reminded me that she and I still needed to talk. I tried to hide behind Regina's dress that she held above her head. She was worried about the white getting dirty, even though it was covered head to toe in plastic. Still, Mrs. Potts spotted me.

"Raevyn!" She yelled for me just before we could get out of the front door.

"Ma'am?" I answered, never stopping. Maybe she would get the hint that I had somewhere to go.

"We still need to talk." She narrowed her eyes at me.

"I haven't forgotten." I tried to smile sweetly, but she didn't return it. She waddled off into the distance without another word.

I caught up with the three of them making haste toward the limo that was stalled at the South gate. Garrison took our bags and we all filed inside, one by one.

"What was that about?" Corrine inquired. "What'd she want?"

"Mrs. Potts is so nosy." Regina shook her head and examined her fingernails. "It's probably not even that big of a deal."

"It's not," I agreed, reaching for one of the four champagne flutes. I needed something to take the heat off me. I knew drinking would keep everyone's mouth shut for a few minutes.

"Atta girl," Andrea cheered and popped the bottle of Moët. She poured orange juice in our glasses and we drank mimosas all the way downtown.

This, I could get used to.

We were pampered and waited on hand and foot, and as the day turned into night I was becoming more and more anxious.

"I can't get over how stunning you look," Corrine gushed, running her hands through my hair. I usually wore it in curls because it was quick and easy to manage. But seeing it straightened, I realized how long my hair was. It nearly reached the middle of my back. My real hair was as long as Andrea's extensions.

I stared at my reflection. I didn't even recognize myself, but I felt more regal than I had in, well, ever. Andrea came into the room, almost naked. She only had on thong underwear. She held her manicured nails over her nipples.

"We need to get dressed," she ordered.

"You especially," I commented, pulling my terry cloth robe around me. She had the most perfect body. I noticed a dark birthmark next to her belly button.

"Oh shut up." She laughed, shimmying her shoulders in my direction.

I covered my eyes playfully. "Stop before you put an eye out with those things."

"Brandon said the limo will be here in fifteen," Corrine announced from a corner of the room where her iPhone was plugged into the wall. "We do need to get dressed," she advised. She stripped off her robe, throwing it in the corner. She too was almost stark naked under it.

"What is with you guys?" I laughed, training my eyes on Regina. She and I were the only two dressed at this point.

Regina cackled and stripped her robe off too. "Oh come on. You might as well too." She turned around and dug for something in her bag. I noticed her tattoo again. It was a pair of ballet slippers. I wondered if that is what prompted her father to outlaw dance in Regina's life.

"We've already seen all that wagon you dragging." Andrea laughed.

"Live a little," Corrine chided.

I studied the three of them, their eyes wide with anticipation. "Fine," I answered. I slowly untied my robe and let it fall to the floor like they had. It did feel good. I felt free.

"See?" Andrea said. "Now we're quadruplets." The four of us cracked up, holding our breasts, bare-naked in a hotel room. I allowed my eyes to scan over the three of them and right then, I genuinely felt like I belonged. I didn't want to be cautious anymore. I wanted to live just a little. I wanted to be a legacy.

We all took a shot of tequila before exiting the limo. My stomach burned like it had been turned inside out. I snuck a swig of water when no one was looking. Jeffrey looked dashing. His fitted tuxedo hugged his lean body. His pocket square matched the ruby red of my floor length, one shoulder Tom Ford dress. I felt like the luckiest girl in the world.

Snow fluttered down in thick flakes, landing lightly on the trim of our fur coats. One landed in the middle of my chest, between the deep V split in my dress that revealed more cleavage that I was comfortable with. I pulled the coat tighter around me. I tried to keep my balance in Regina's Jimmy Choo heels as we walked up the hill to the estate, looping the train of my dress around my finger. Jeffrey braced me when I stumbled. If he wasn't here I would have fallen flat on my face by now. The strappy heels were pinching both of my baby toes and it was slowly but surely becoming unbearable. Regina promised once we got inside and had a few drinks I wouldn't be able to feel my feet anymore. To her, a drink solved everything.

The small hill, lined with identical manicured bushes atop a stone wall that ascended in height until we reached the mansion. I squeezed Jeffrey's arm when it came into full view. Only superstars on TV lived in homes like these. And here I was, walking into one.

The house was made entirely of stone and illuminated by built-in spotlights. The soft beat of jazz music floated out into the night. I could see throngs of people moving harmoniously through each room inside. My heart was drumming nervously, and I wondered if Jeffrey could hear it. He looked down at me and discreetly kissed my forehead. I immediately looked for Regina but she was already inside.

A butler greeted us. "Jeffrey Vincent Eugene Donnelly the fourth," Jeffrey said confidently, presenting his invitation. "And Raevyn Elizabeth Jones, my guest." I hesitantly handed over my invitation. I was hoping to keep it. He dropped them into a bucket beside him allowing entry into the home.

A few steps ahead Regina, Brandon, Andrea, and Corrine waited for us. Another member of the wait staff came over and pulled our coats off our shoulders. He tagged the coat and handed me a ticket. Corrine smiled brightly at me.

"Cool, right?" she mouthed, taking a look around and I nodded back towards her. This was more than cool. We were the youngest faces in the crowd and still no one stopped us. We looked like we belonged.

The marble foyer opened up into a large family room. The vaulted ceilings and sparse furniture made the room seem like it could swallow B. W. Fitz whole. I couldn't believe a person that looked like me owned this. This was the definition of Black Excellence. This was what all those posters prompted us to be. I wondered if this was what my father missed out on. Could we have had exclusive parties like this? Could we have lived in this house? I would have never seen anything like this had I stayed in

Maryland and for a split second I was appreciative that my dad sent me away.

A woman dressed in a tuxedo made her way over to us.

"Welcome to the Mason estate." She smiled, presenting us with a flute of bubbling champagne. We all reached for a glass without hesitation.

"To a perfect night." Regina raised her glass in the air.

"A perfect night indeed," Jeffrey agreed. I didn't need anything more.

The music drowned out and a hush fell over the crowd. We turned our attention to a brown skinned woman in a mid-length turquoise dress that complemented her bronze skin. Her dark hair cascaded down her bony shoulders in soft waves. She approached the microphone and beckoned for someone to join her. Reluctantly a light skinned, tall, bald man joined her at the microphone. He wrapped his arms around her waist and pecked her on the cheek. The crowd whooped at the romantic gesture. She fanned her hand in the crowd's direction and her huge diamond ring caught the light. I wondered how she even kept a rock like that on such a small finger.

"Doctor Mason and I want to thank you all for attending our Christmas gala this year." She allowed her husband to snuggle his face in the crook of her neck. "As you can see, someone is elated to be out of the hospital."

A laugh rippled through the crowd. "On behalf of my family…" She beckoned for someone else to join her. A little girl in a frilly pink dress joined her mother. Dr. Mason reached down for his daughter and placed her on his hip. She draped her skinny arms around his neck automatically and brought her thumb to her mouth, resting her long, platted hair on her father's shoulder. My heart expanded at the sight. I missed my dad.

A younger boy not much older than his sister shuffled on the stage, tugging at his bow tie and clutching his mother's hand. Finally an older male approached. I had to do a double take because I thought I recognized him. It might have been how blinding the spotlight was but after scanning his face once more I realized I did recognize him. In fact, I knew him.

"Your boyfriend didn't say he was a Mason," Jeffrey accused, never taking his eyes off Dre. "I knew I knew him from somewhere."

"Because he isn't," I mumbled.

Dr. Mason clapped his hand on Dre's back. His dreadlocks brushed his shoulders and he waved to the crowd like he belonged.

Andrea turned to us and whispered, "I know where I'll be spending the rest of my night."

Regina smirked, downing her champagne. "Snagging a Mason is like catching Big Foot, girl. You can try all your life but they are hard to get a hold of. Once you do, I heard it's unbelievable."

"Does he go to Fitz?" Andrea asked, never taking her eyes off Dre as if she just settled on her prey.

"All Masons attend Morehouse. Unless you plan on moving to Atlanta, I suggest you forget it." Regina shrugged, picking a hors d'oeuvre off a passing tray. Her eyes settled on Jeffrey and me. "And you *know* how they are in Atlanta."

"Try a crab ball," she suggested to the group before stalking off. Andrea scurried off behind her and Corrine started in the same direction when Brandon stopped her. He whispered something in her ear that made her cheeks turn rosy and they both sauntered away from the group.

I was still in shock to say much of anything. Andre was a Mason? What else did he lie to me about?

"Want to get out of here?" Jeffrey whispered to me, acknowledging my shocked state.

I shook my head. "No."

A tray passed and I took Regina's advice. I grabbed a crab ball and popped it into my mouth. Jeffrey grabbed our champagne flutes and we downed them all at once. I felt it mix with the tequila. "I'm cool."

"Want another?" he asked as a waitress moved swiftly through the crowd with a tray of flutes. He made the motion that he could reach out to grab one.

"Water, please."

Jeffrey placed his hand on the small of my back. A zip of heat shot through my bones when he leaned into me. His lips grazed my ear lightly, electrifyingly, as he said, "Be right back."

As much as I wanted to stay and have a perfect night with Jeffrey, I needed to find Dre. Why did he lie about being a Mason? Why did he lie to me at all? I scanned the crowd, looking for other young faces. I spotted him conversing with people here and there as he moved through the mass.

I hiked up my dress and moved across the room toward him, dipping around dancing couples until I was only feet away. He was speaking with an older woman who was dripping in diamonds. She clutched his arm and spoke incessantly about her granddaughter being perfect for a guy like him. He smiled back at her politely, trying ever so slightly to relinquish her ninja grip.

He turned his head in my direction, giving me his fake, plastered smile as if I was just another patron at this party, waiting for my chance to speak with him. But once he recognized me, I saw a wave of guilt crash down around him. I wasn't exactly giving him a pleasant smile either. He ripped his arm away from the older woman, who stumbled backwards, calling after him, "Andre!" He ignored her, barreling towards me.

"Oh, nice to see your first name isn't a lie too," I snapped.

"What are you doing here?" Dre growled. He kept a smile on his face for passersby who greeted him welcomingly, or commented on how delicious the food was.

"I was invited, Mr. Mason." I made sure to add emphasis on his real last name.

"It's not what you think." He took me by the arm and led me out of the living room to a quieter hallway.

Pictures of the Mason family through their several life stages hung on the wall. A few people were standing around admiring them, pointing from the picture back to Dre, oohing and ahhing.

"How did you get in here?"

"You lied to me," I retorted.

"Not on purpose." He dug his hands deep into the crisp pockets of his tailored white suit. "I knew if you knew that I was a Mason you'd never talk to me."

"So all that crap about you being from New Orleans and speaking fluent French is a lie? You've been lying to me this whole time?"

"I didn't lie to you!" he screamed. An older woman whose dress was too small for her breasts looked between Dre and me, suspiciously. She tapped the guy next to her on the shoulder, who turned. The pair leaned in, pretending they weren't listening.

"Give us a minute," Dre spat. His eyes never wavered from mine. The people in the hallway abandoned their personal missions, conversations died, and everyone dispersed immediately as if the room had been set on fire.

"Some authority you got there." I moved across the hall, leaning on the opposite wall. "You say jump, people jump. Impressive."

"Raevyn." Dre ran his hand through his dreadlocks and scrubbed his face as if he was waiting for a lie to drop into his mind. I hated him for lying to me. And I hated him even more for looking so good while he did it. "You don't understand. You weren't supposed to be here."

"You mean I was never supposed to know, right?"

"No one was supposed to know," he hissed. "Listen, everyone knows my family. So when you told me you didn't know my name, I was shocked. Everywhere I go people know who I am. People give me anything I want not because of who I am, but because of who my parents are."

"Boo hoo," I jeered.

He sucked his teeth. "I begged my parents to let me go to B. W. Fitz instead of Morehouse. I didn't want to be Andre Mason of *the* Mason brigade. I wanted to make my own legacy."

"Oh, such a hard life." I yawned, patting my mouth dramatically. I started to walk away when he stepped in front of me.

"Move," I ordered.

"No one can find out, Raevyn. Please do this for me," he begged. But I was too angry to sympathize for anyone who lied about living in a house as amazing as this one.

"All that shit…" I chuckled. Memories of our long talks and even our shared quiet moments flashed through my mind.

"All that shit you told me about being different. 'You get me.'" I mocked his voice. "That was all a lie? All of my friends just saw you get announced as a Mason. You think no one at Fitz is going to find out now? How are you going to keep this lie up, Mr. Mason?"

"You're going to make sure they don't find out unless you want Professor Bonhomme to know how you aced all those French exams. You *need* me, Raevyn."

Blood shot through my veins. My heart pumped double time, pulsing out of my ears. I dug around in my purse until I found my—his—iPhone. I chucked it against the wall just missing the side of his face. The glass shattered into a million pieces. It matched how my heart felt.

"I don't need a goddamn thing from you, Andre Mason."

The limousine felt like it was swerving in and out of the highway lanes. Every few seconds I felt my stomach flip up and down, in and out, front and back again.

My head felt like a construction zone, like someone was jack hammering at my temples. After my fight with Dre I didn't know how many shots I took. I just wanted to forget even meeting him. It felt like I lost Antoine all over again.

Everything happened so quickly. I remember throwing up in a flowerbed, and Jeffrey calling a limo service, but everything else in between was a blur.

I crumpled into the seat letting my head cool against the icy window.

"You don't need him," Jeffrey managed to say. It sounded like his tongue was swollen. "You're too good for him." He relaxed his head against the back of the seat.

"Thanks, Jeffrey." I sniffed.

"Y- you need me. I – I can take better care of you." He hiccupped.

I sat up and the hammering returned fiercely. The lights from the highway passed over his face and I thought I could see him smiling. I debated on asking him to repeat himself. Given my state I could have very well imagined it.

"What'd you say?" I squeaked.

"I said come 'ere."

I scrambled over to Jeffrey before he could change his mind and dropped onto him clumsily.

"Rae." He groaned. "You're on my bladder." He pulled me close, flipping me on my back, cradling my body.

I kicked off Regina's Jimmy Choo stilettos and allowed myself to relax safely in his arms, breathing in his cologne. Before long I heard his soft snores. Even though my stomach felt as though I'd eaten sixteen tubs of Jell-O, and there was a fifty percent chance that this was just a dream, I'd do it all again to lie here with Jeffrey.

The limo screeched to a halt and ceiling lights flooded the interior. Cold air rushed into the car and cackles broke the silence—loud, insufferable cackles that I recognized from none other than Corrine.

"Hey," she practically screamed, slapping my arm. Everything felt magnified. "Wake up!"

"What is it?" I turned my back to her, away from the harsh lights that stabbed at my eyes.

"We're at McDonald's. What do you want?"

"I'm not hungry," I growled. "Close the freaking door."

"You need food, dipshit." She slapped my arm again. "Wake up!"

"Chicken nuggets!" I screamed at the top of my lungs. "For God's sake, get me some chicken nuggets. Twenty piece."

"You're going to eat twenty chicken nuggets?" She scoffed.

"For Jeffrey," I mumbled.

A pair of heels click-clacked on the pavement. A giggle accompanied those heels. It was Andrea. "Regina!" she shrieked.

Another pair of heels scurried over. I wanted to lift myself out of Jeffrey's lap, but I was too weak to move.

"She said a twenty piece for Jeff," Corrine reported.

"Jeffrey doesn't even eat McDonald's," Regina said in a quiet, knowing voice.

"Get the twenty piece," I demanded, reaching for the door handle. "It's his favorite." I slammed the door closed, letting the heat re-circulate inside. Andrea's screams faded farther and farther away as our limo pulled away. I settled back into Jeffrey's body. He leaned toward me and I felt his warm lips meet my forehead.

"We're in big trouble when we get back to campus," he mumbled.

"We can worry about that after the nuggets." I pushed myself closer to him and soon after fell peacefully asleep.

The next day I woke up to the sun beaming directly into my window. The rays felt like they were piercing my eyes, sending a shooting pain to my brain. I sat up and the desk slid across the floor. Then the chair followed and then the closet. I cradled my forehead, thinking I could venture across the room to shut the curtain but nothing stayed still long enough.

My phone vibrated. I felt around blindly under my covers, fumbling over stray chicken nuggets and jewelry, until I found it. Everything from last night came flooding back to me all at once. Dre somehow managed to find me after our argument and slip the phone back in my bag. The shattered glass scratched my finger when I slid my thumb across the screen to unlock the phone.

I read Corrine's text with one eye open.

Breakfast at 9.

I glanced over at my bedside table clock. It was 8:15 a.m. and if I didn't get a move on now I would surely be late.

I slowly texted her back.

What happened last night? I feel horrible.

U drank 2 much. Tell u @ breakfast. Reggie is pissed.

Great, I responded.

I willed myself to get up. I slinked along the wall until I reached the bathroom. I popped two Tylenol and hopped in the shower. The hot water beat down on my skin working wonders for my hangover. I threw on a FITZ tee and a pair of Seven jeans. I stuffed my feet in a pair of tall tan Ugg boots and pulled on my Chanel hat. It fit so much better now that my hair was straightened.

I crossed the living room to Regina's door and knocked, but there was no answer. I tried the handle and the door was locked. She must've already left.

It was a beautiful, sunny winter morning and campus was bustling. The sun made the fresh snow glisten beautifully. People dragged suitcases from their dorms, waving goodbye to their friends before hopping in waiting limos or jumping behind the wheel of the latest Mercedes. I remembered today was the official start of Christmas break. Everyone was heading home.

Everyone except me.

I maneuvered my way through the crowds of students and a part of me wished I was going away, too. But I knew I had nothing to go home to. An eerily empty cafeteria greeted me and I immediately jumped in the omelette line.

"What can I get for ya?" A man in a greasy uniform leaned on the counter. Sweat clung to his forehead while he rocked two steaming frying pans back and forth over the stove.

"Uh..." I consulted the menu next to him. The edges of the page had yellowed from years of complacency. I rocked back on my heels. "I'll take the veggie omelette."

"You got it, pretty lady," the man replied. He flipped a towel out of his apron and dabbed at his forehead. The ends of his fingers were dark like he'd burned them several times over.

When he replaced the towel I got a glimpse at his name tag, Gary.

He whistled a happy song while he worked. He and I waited while a handful of spinach wilted in the pan. "I ain't never seen you before." He crossed his arms. "You new?"

"Yeah," I answered. "Mrs. Potts said to try your omelettes, so here I am."

The corners of his mouth lifted into a crooked smile. "That lady loves my cookin'." He tossed a handful of vegetables in the pan and he spoke over the sizzle. He reminded me of a guy in my neighborhood, Mr. James. He was a jack-of-all-trades. He could install a toilet and change the oil on your car all in the same day. He could talk for hours about anything in the world, from pop culture to police brutality, to politics, all while a limp cigarette hung from his lips.

"So, where you from?"

"Maryland." The smell of food made my stomach growl with longing. My headache drummed in my temples. I leaned on the counter to keep myself upright. He picked up the pan, holding it out to me.

"Gon' head," he prompted. "I know you been thinking about it. I can read the hangover all over your face." I plucked a few mushrooms out of the pan. They singed my fingers when I threw them into my mouth. He tossed in a handful of ham and bacon. "You need some fat to soak up that liquor, gal." I sputtered out a laugh. I couldn't believe it was that obvious.

"You're probably right."

He spun around and cracked a few eggs in a bowl, whisking furiously while glancing over his shoulder, keeping a close eye on the vegetables. I noticed a number, 94, tattooed behind his ear. I wondered what it meant.

"How long you been working here?" I asked.

"A long time," he answered, spinning back around, dumping the eggs in the pan. He started whistling again while the eggs cooked. He eyed me for a second before saying, "You say you from Maryland, huh?"

"Well," I hesitated. I wanted to correct myself, but I knew it was too late. I had to go with it now. "Yeah."

"You look like someone I know." He flipped the omelette. "Someone I haven't seen in a long time."

"Who?"

"Ain't no way you'd know him." He smiled, like he was visiting a memory. "A guy named Chuck, graduated in '94."

"Chuck Jones?" I asked with a thumping heart.

"Yeah." He plated my omelette. Silence crossed the room and he took a long look at me again. "Are you...you ain't Chuck's little girl, is you?"

"I'm Raevyn Jones. Char—well, Chuck's little girl." I beamed.

"Well ain't this nothing." He clapped his hands together, sprinting from behind the counter. He scooped me up in his arms before I could protest and hugged me until it felt like my ribs would crack in half, or until I threw up everything in my stomach. His eyes glistened with tears as he said, "You let me know if you ever need anything, all right? Anything at all."

Taken aback and woozy I managed to point at my plate. "I'll take my omelette."

"You got it." He clapped his hands and sprinkled an illegal amount of cheese on top before sliding my plate across the counter.

Reeling, I bowed out of the room.

When I approached the table, the talking immediately ceased. Brandon looked up at me embarrassedly and put his head back down into a book. I took my normal seat by Jeffrey and he ran his hand up the thigh of my jeans. I tried extremely hard to hide my smile and greet everyone.

Andrea didn't respond, flicking the pages of her magazine. Regina kept her eyes glued to the screen of her phone. I looked over at Corrine who mouthed the words, "Told you."

"What's going on?" I asked the group.

Regina looked up at me, she rolled her eyes, and began typing again. Andrea dramatically flicked a page and it fell gracefully into the others.

"Is it about last night?"

"I'm not hungry anymore," Regina announced. She grabbed her perspiring frappuccino from the table and stood up. "Andrea, what time is Garrison coming?"

"Around ten," she answered, gathering her stuff too.

"Good, maybe I'll have some time to hang out with my *real* friends before leaving."

Brandon sucked his teeth. "Stop being so dramatic, Reggie," he scolded. "You act like the girl stole your boyfriend."

"Excuse me?" I cut in.

Regina shot Brandon a cold look and said, "Corrine, Andrea, are you ready?"

They trailed behind her as she stole out of the cafeteria.

"What the hell was that about?" I asked, finally digging into my omelette. My mouth watered in anticipation.

"Jeffrey is Regina's Jack." Brandon sighed.

"Her what?" I asked, rolling the piping hot eggs around in my mouth.

"Her Jack," Jeffrey repeated as if I hadn't heard Brandon the first time.

"What's that mean?"

Bandon and Jeffrey exchanged puzzled glances before looking over at me again. Was this something I was supposed to know?

"Her Jack," Brandon started. "You know, Jack and Jill."

"Basically, she's the girl I'm supposed to marry. Her family selected me a while ago to be the Jack to Regina's Jill. You've never heard of Jack and Jill before?"

My stomach dropped to my feet. "No."

"Wait, wait," Jeffrey scoffed.

"Aren't you a legacy?" Brandon leaned over.

Jeffrey talked over Brandon's question. "She gets jealous when she sees me with other girls because everyone knows I'm her Jack."

"And she's your Jill." I was starting to understand but it didn't make my stomach feel any better.

"Exactly," Brandon said. He placed a bookmark on the page he was studying. "So when she saw you two last night, she flipped."

I swallowed and poked at my eggs. I wasn't hungry anymore.

"You want to marry her?"

"I don't have a choice." Jeffrey shrugged. "When we graduate, Regina will probably work here. I'll go to law school and we'll get married. That's just the way it goes."

"That doesn't seem unfair to you?" I asked, trying not to seem so disappointed. It made me wonder if last night meant anything to him. If he was supposed to be with Regina why wasn't he with her now? Why did he say I needed him? Why did he kiss me? Why was he even interested in me at all if he had Little-Miss-Perfect?

"That's how it's done." Brandon shrugged. "Well-to-do families marry other well-to-do families. We don't have a choice in the matter."

I suddenly felt like such an idiot. Why hadn't I seen it before? The way Regina would be so rude to me when I talked about Jeffrey. She was only protecting her property. I could never be with Jeffrey because he was already chosen.

"What's your legacy again?" Brandon inquired.

"I should go apologize," I cut him off. "I didn't know."

I bolted from the table leaving the two of them to their thoughts. I made sure not to look at Jeffrey when I left.

There was so much about being a legacy I didn't know. What else was I supposed to know that my dad neglected to tell me? It seemed like every time I settled into the notion that I belonged here, something else made me stick out again.

Once I reached my dorm, Mrs. Potts was standing cross-legged in the foyer. I wasn't in the emotional state to have a conversation with her. She blocked the entrance to the elevator so I had no choice but to talk to her now.

"Morning," I mumbled, hoping to rush past her but I knew she wasn't going to let me by without having this conversation. She'd been trying for weeks now.

"Raevyn, I've been trying to catch up with you and you've been ducking me." I wasn't really ducking her; I've just been taking the stairs instead of the elevator in hopes not to see her, two totally different things. "So I'm just gonna come right out and say it. I don't think you should converse with people like that."

"People like what?"

"I accepted charges from a *prison*," she emphasized. "Now, I see you got a cell phone and all, so I don't expect any more calls from those kinds of people coming here, correct?"

Her words could have knocked me off my feet. "Those kinds of people?" I repeated, trying to process what she was saying to me. Those...kinds...of...people.

She nodded, stressing her point. "You're stepping into something bigger and better and you don't need to be bogged down with...criminals." She crossed her arms over her chest waving her hand when she said the word criminals as if Antoine was a spec of dirt in the air.

"Bogged down with criminals, huh?" I echoed. She didn't even know Antoine. How dare she. I took a few deep breaths in attempts to calm myself down.

"Exactly. I'm glad you see it my way."

"Oh, I see it perfectly." I pushed past her and jabbed the button for the elevator. She watched me until I boarded, looking so pleased with herself.

I could have punched a hole in the wall. People like Antoine and I weren't born with silver spoons in our mouths. We had to hustle out of desperation. We didn't have legacies and trust funds and living rooms the size of amusement parks. One thing was for sure, just because the people at B. W. Fitz had more money that sure didn't make up for their lack of common courtesy.

I flung open the door to my room and saw Corrine, Andrea, and Regina sprawled out on the couch. Suitcases and carry-on bags littered the room. They all sat up swiftly when I stormed in.

"Listen, Reggie," I demanded. "I didn't know Jeffrey was your Jack, okay?"

"You didn't know?" Andrea hopped up. "Everyone knows!"

"Guys, maybe she genuinely didn't know," Corrine expressed. "There were tons of things I didn't know."

"Oh, Corrine please," Regina exclaimed.

"You guys don't even like each other!" I shouted.

"That's not the point," she responded. "Jeffrey is the man I'm going to marry, Raevyn. It's as simple as that. Like Andrea said, everyone here knows that."

"Everyone, except you, obviously," Andrea chimed in. "Jones Funeral home in Atlanta," she scoffed. "Yeah, right."

"You think I'm lying?" I crossed the room and stood directly in front of Andrea. I was tired of her and everyone else here who thought they were better than me just because their bank account had more zeroes. "Come right out and say it." I challenged her.

"Yes, I think you're lying. I don't know how you got in, Raevyn," Andrea stated, "but it's not because you're a legacy. Maybe you're on scholarship."

Regina cackled in the background.

"That's why you have to work in the gym. Who knows," she said nonchalantly. She whipped her hair backwards and locked her eyes on to mine. I knew if I hit her I would be expelled. I would be back in Maryland with no hope of a future. I would be playing right into their game.

"Andrea, don't." Corrine pleaded, looking between Andrea, Regina, and me. "It was an honest mistake."

"I want my blazer back, scholarship student." Regina sneered, ignoring Corrine.

I wheeled around, marched into my room, and ripped her blazer off the hanger.

"Take it." I threw her Prada boots and her Jimmy Choo shoes at her feet too.

"Rae, stop!" Corrine screamed. She pulled herself off the floor and ran over to me. I slammed the door in her face before she got too close.

"Leave me alone," I ordered.

"Well," I heard Andrea announce. "No Turks and Caicos for you."

"She has to stay through the break anyway," Regina commented. "She couldn't come if we wanted her to."

"See you 'round, scholarship student," Andrea taunted. I jumped when I heard something smack my bedroom door. They rustled around for a bit and then I heard the door to the suite open and slam shut.

The campus of Benjamin Wallace Fitzgerald was a ghost town during Christmas break. I didn't realize how accustomed I'd grown to having Regina, Andrea, and Corrine around. I did everything alone. Now, when I thought about the three of them, anger overpowered all the good memories we had.

I added Dre's name to the list of ruined friendships I accumulated during the semester, too. He and I hadn't spoken since the Mason ball. He hadn't once tried to contact me and it made me wonder if he ever meant all the things he said anyway. I was grateful that Christmas break started right after the ball but everything ended so quickly. It was almost as if we never existed to each other. Did friendships mean anything to these people? It seemed as if everything could be tossed away; nothing here was genuine.

Without Regina, Andrea, and Corrine distracting me I managed to catch up on most of my work. My papers and homework assignments were getting completed on time and by the end of Christmas break, I predicted that I would be on track with the rest of my classmates.

Corrine would call me sometimes when Andrea and Regina weren't around. She'd tell me about Turks and Caicos and how she wished that I could have joined them. She said as soon as they left that day, Regina and Andrea didn't speak about the situation anymore. She hoped when we all reunited at school next year everything would be okay. I loved Corrine's optimism, but knowing Andrea and Regina, they didn't strike me as the type to forget so easily.

It had only been about two weeks since they left. If I hadn't forgotten, then I knew they didn't either. I didn't know how it would be once they arrived back on campus, but I hoped it wouldn't be so awkward for Corrine.

Ever since Andrea accused me of being a scholarship student, I began to wonder about my own legacy. Who were the Jones's in Atlanta and how did my father know them? There were about fifty Jones Funeral Homes in Atlanta when I searched for it on Google. It was too tedious to sort through all the information.

I bought a new iPhone as a Christmas gift to myself and I wanted more than anything to call my dad. I knew it would be a bad idea, but still, on Christmas morning, I did it anyway. He answered on the first ring. My heart jumped when I heard his husky voice. He must have been just waking up.

"Dad," I spoke through sobs that clawed at my heart.

"Raevyn?" he whispered back.

"Merry Christmas." I laughed. When my cheeks rose the tears trickled down, landing with a splash on my laptop keyboard. I noticed the screen scramble a little before returning to its regular state. I immediately saved everything I was working on in case the whole thing crashed.

"Merry Christmas, baby," he responded. I could tell he was trying to keep his composure too. "You know we can't..." he started. I knew what he was going to say. He was going to say that we couldn't stay on the phone for long.

"I know." I cut him off. The images distorted on my monitor again and seconds later, it was normal again. I shut down my laptop and pushed it from me. Maybe it was overheating. "I had to wish my dad a Merry Christmas. I miss you guys."

"We miss you too, every single day, baby." I heard rustling on the other end of the phone.

"How is Mom? How's the recovery program going?"

My dad sighed heavily before answering. "She's...doing better. We are taking it slow, one step at a time."

"Has she been going to her meetings?"

"I take her every week. She's starting to gain a bit of weight back, too. Everything is steady, Rae."

"I know you're taking good care of her, Dad." I wished I were there with my family rather than holed up in my dorm room, eating lukewarm macaroni and cheese and a couple slices of cold ham. I'd give anything to be eating popcorn, snuggled on our ratty couch with my dad. If my mom were feeling well she would normally fall asleep while he and I watched *How the Grinch Stole Christmas* over and over again. It hurt knowing that I took all those times for granted. I'd never get that back now.

"How are you liking Fitz?"

"It's interesting to say the least, Chuck." I teased.

"Ahhh, you must have met Ralphie." He chuckled. "She's a piece of work, that one."

"Dad, how come you didn't tell me about all this? About all these people that knew you back then. How come you never told me about this legacy?" I hugged a pillow to my chest, relaxing my head against my headboard. Although it wasn't the ideal circumstance I was happy to speak to someone who knew me, the real me, inside and out. For weeks, all I'd wanted was my daddy.

"It's hard to explain," he began. "I–I didn't know what to say, honestly. I knew you'd question things. I just want you to have the experience of a lifetime like I did. You deserve that. You deserve nice things and opportunities. I can't give you that here. I've tried. I knew you had to go to Fitz to get it."

"I went to the Mason ball with my friends and it made me wonder. What happened? Why didn't you stay here? Was our legacy not good enough?"

He paused and said, "You went...where?" I noticed his voice changed. It was no longer loving and fatherly. He wasn't laughing anymore. He was angry. He was *very* angry.

"The Mason ball," I repeated softly.

"What did I tell you before I left? You keep your nose clean and stay out of trouble, right?"

I imagined his angry vein throbbing in his forehead. Before Mom relapsed again she was the authoritative figure. My dad was usually the one who gave me anything I wanted. But when Mom could no longer deal with reality, Dad assumed the role. Ever since, it kind of just...stuck. Sometimes, I despised my mother for taking my fun-loving dad away from me. All that was left now was his angry vein.

"Trouble? Dad! It was just a dance!" I neglected to tell him about the drinking.

"I have to go," he responded. "Your mother is up. You do your work and you go home, you got that? Nothing, and I mean nothing, in between."

"Dad, please," I begged. "I need to know."

"Stay from 'round those people and out of trouble. I have to go," he insisted before I heard the phone click on the other end.

I slammed my phone down on the bed and turned my attention back to my defective computer. I powered it on and the welcome screen sang its normal song. Before long, I was typing again, totally consumed in my political science final.

When I opened my email a window flashed announcing a new message from someone named B. There was no subject. My first instinct was to mark it as spam, but I opened it anyway. It read:

New girl – get out now.

Beside me, my phone beeped with a new text message that said the same thing as the email. I replied: **Who is this?**

A message came back immediately stating the user was blocked. A chill slipped over my skin. I fought through my initial thoughts of fear. My mind slowed and I realized this wasn't a threat. Corrine thought Regina and Andrea had forgotten, but I didn't. I knew this was their way of playing a cruel joke on me. They knew I wasn't a legacy and wanted me to go back home.

I wasn't caving that easily. I wasn't afraid of anyone or anything especially not a stupid text message. They would have to work a little harder to get me to leave.

⚬⟋⟍⟋⟍⟋⟍⟋⟍⟋⟍⟋⟍⟋⟍⟍⟍⟍⟍⟍⟋⟍⟍⟍⟋⟍⟋⟍⟋⟍⟋⟍⟍⟍⟍⟍⟋⟍⟋⟍⟋⟍⟍⟋⟍⟍⟋⟍⟍⟋⟍⟋⟍⟍⟍⟍⟍⟋⟍⟍⟍⟍⟍⟍⟋⟍⟍⟍⟍⟍⟍⟍⟍⟍⟋⟍⟍⟋⟍⟍⟋⟍⟍⟋⟍⟍⟋⟍⟍⟍⟋⟍⟍⟍

Time passed agonizingly slow. Days began to melt together. I was so bored after my assignments were done that I started an exercise regimen of all things. I went on long jogs around the campus. Because Fitz was so big each run was a new adventure.

The east side of campus by the senior honors dormitories was still undiscovered. By the time I got over there I finally understood why everyone wanted to belong to the exclusive white blazer society at B. W. Fitz. It was almost like a new world.

I slowed when I approached a luxury apartment style building. The balconies were crowded with snow-covered grills that had been abandoned in the winter months. Plants grew out wildly, brown and wilted, and the seats of matching patio furniture were soaked with snow. The seniors had their own cafeteria and even a small field of grass that probably served as their courtyard in the summer months.

A gazebo sat beyond the dormitories overlooking a frozen lake. My legs screamed for mercy and I obeyed their requests. I flopped down on the bench in the gazebo, which was surprisingly warm. Heat curled around my legs and when I felt around for the source I heard someone say, "Heated benches."

Startled, I looked up and noticed Headmaster Randolph sitting on the opposite end. His frail body wrapped tightly in a black coat that skimmed the gazebo's floor.

"I had them installed last year," he continued, looking out onto the surface of the lake. He took a deep sigh. "I think it's one of the best investments I've made in all my years here."

He looked over at me, and his lips curved slowly into a smile. The wrinkled skin around his brown eyes pinched together and made his glasses teeter on the edge of his nose.

"I didn't know anyone else was out here." I wrung my hands over each other. I'd never been so close to him before. He seemed so regal, so untouchable when he gave the morning announcements. What should I say?

"It helps me think," he responded.

A couple of birds danced around on the banister in front of us. They pecked at something before making the decision to fly away. Headmaster Randolph smiled at their antics, watching them until the two birds disappeared in the overcast sky.

His eyes slid over to me. "Do you run a lot in Maryland?"

"Sir?" I tried to clear my throat but it had gone dry completely. My heart stomped around in my chest.

"It's okay," he assured me. "I was the Headmaster during your father's years, ya know. So when he called about you I made sure you got what you needed."

"You...know my father?"

He looked at me for a long while. It wasn't an uncomfortable stare. It was a probing one, as if he could see through me, like he was watching my life story on a reel. He glanced down at his hands and then back out at the lake.

"Your father is one of the noblest men I know besides that Terry Rudd." He pointed over his shoulder in the opposite direction. "I'm proud to say I know the both of them." He glanced up at me quickly and I thought I saw tears glisten in his eyes.

My father? All at once, questions about my dad blossomed in my mind. "Sir? Can I ask you something?"

"Shoot." He dabbed at his eyes with the back of his trembling hand. He should be inside.

"What happened to my father?" His eyebrows knit together quickly. "Am I really a legacy like he said?"

"Certainly." He nodded.

"Then why did he leave here? Why don't I know anything about this place?"

He struggled to his feet, pushing his breath slowly through his teeth. He pulled a cane out from beside him and made his way in short, confident strides toward me.

"I'm afraid I can't give you the answers to your questions, Raevyn. You'll have to ask him yourself." He pushed his glasses up on his nose.

"But—"

"It's more complicated than you know. He'll tell you at the right time." With that he meandered out of the gazebo and followed the paved trail that snaked around the lake and back toward campus.

I had it in my mind to follow him but I knew I wouldn't get anywhere. My father either did something miraculous or something he was very ashamed of and no one would breathe a word.

Christmas season churned into the New Year and in about a week the campus would be buzzing with students once again. I went back to the lake almost every day since speaking with Headmaster Randolph, hoping to see him, but he never returned. He must have known I would return, too. I deserved to know what everyone else knew about my father. What was he hiding?

My inbox was overrun with text messages and emails from B. They were all the same message: **Get out now.** Seriously, Andrea and Regina were both college educated. They couldn't come up with anything better than that? A small part of me wondered, though, what if the messages weren't from Regina or Andrea? Who else would want me out of here so badly?

I tried not to concentrate on that or anything else but it was hard to keep my brain from wandering in the quiet times I spent by myself in my room.

Instead, I focused all of my energy on my GPA. I only had one grade left that determined whether I would stay in the pre-honors program. Professor Carmichael. And I had a strange feeling he knew that everything depended on his grade. Maybe he was B.

I couldn't help but laugh at that while I swam in the pool one day at work. The gym was empty since everyone left for break and I had to do something to pass the time on my shifts. I'd been eating horribly over the break, stuff that I wouldn't touch during the semester under Regina's watchful eye. Exhausted, with rubbery arms, I pulled myself up and sat on the sidewall when I heard a set of footsteps approaching. I whipped around and Jeffrey swaggered over. I could tell the outline of his body even with foggy goggles.

"Do you always swim on your shifts?" I pulled my goggles off and took in his usual uniform—a sweater, bow tie, and pressed pants. I tried to suppress my grin and the urge to sprint into his arms. I didn't care if he really was Regina's property. I needed his embrace. I needed to smell him. I needed to feel him.

"Just to pass the time," I answered, adjusting my bathing suit. I wondered how long he'd been standing there watching me swim.

"Well aren't you going to give me a hug?" His velvety voice echoed around the room, amplifying it times a hundred, penetrating the walls of my heart.

"I'm soaking wet, Jeff."

"So, is that a no?"

"You want a hug that bad?" I laughed, but inside, my heart was doing somersaults. "Let me dry off first, okay?"

I went to move around him but he grabbed my hand, spinning me around and embracing me tightly. I was swept up in his familiar fragrance, of clean, fresh musk. I wanted to feel him, to smell him, to see him for so long. I fell into his familiar body, and my knees turned to putty.

"Don't fight it," he whispered playfully in my ear.

I pulled away, regretful that he could feel how much I needed him. "What are you doing here?"

"I'm the assistant dean of students," he reminded me. "Dr. Rudd flies me in a week early and we take care of the administrative stuff. Mostly boring paperwork."

"Oh, so you can tell me what I got on Carmichael's paper?" I asked, pulling my cap off my head. I watched Jeffrey's eyes while he watched my hair flow down around my shoulders.

"Sure, I can tell you." He shrugged seemingly unfazed. "Is it your final paper?"

"Yeah," I answered. "It's keeping me from whether I stay in the pre-honors program."

"Want to put some clothes on?" He pointed over my shoulder toward the locker rooms. "We can run to Dr. Rudd's office right now."

I scoffed in disbelief. "I was just playing. You can really see grades?"

"It's no big deal, Rae." Jeffrey glanced at his watch. "Dr. Rudd is gone, it's past seven. I know his passwords. We'll log in, check it out, and get back out of there. Easy as pie."

I narrowed my eyes at him. "And what do you want in return?"

"Is that a serious question?"

"You're off limits, Jeffrey. Why are you even doing this for me?" I knew it was too soon to get into this argument, but I hadn't heard from him all break. Now he shows up looking all delicious at my job. How unfair is that? I wasn't prepared. I at least would have put on some real clothes.

He rubbed the back of his neck while another hand dug deep into his pants pocket.

"I see you haven't forgotten about that. That's another reason I came back early. I needed to see you. We need to talk."

"See me? We can't hang out." My anger finally bubbled to the surface. I began to list on my fingers. "We can't even be seen with each other. I mean if I come within two inches of you, I get threatening text messages or I'm attacked by your pit bulls."

"Texts? Pit bulls?" His face twisted. "What are you talking about?"

"Don't play stupid with me, Jeffrey."

He turned his palms out to me. "I don't know what you're talking about. I left for Turks and Caicos with them and about halfway to the airport I realized you weren't coming."

"Oh, nothing at breakfast that morning told you that I wasn't coming?" He couldn't expect me to believe that. Who did he think I was? Corrine? How could he just think everything would be okay? He wasn't sad that we couldn't be together? He thought I was cool with accepting Regina's dibs on him? Has he forgotten everything that happened between us?

"Raevyn, calm down," Jeffrey demanded in a stern voice, one that I never heard before. How could he be mad at me? "Go put some clothes on and we can talk about this." I refused to move. I wasn't obeying his orders.

"Either we're talking about this now, or we're not talking at all." I crossed my arms over my chest. He would have to do this on my terms, not his. Even though I wanted to get dressed because the cold air seemed to be seeping into my bones, I wasn't giving in that easily.

"Raevyn Elizabeth Jones," Jeffrey boomed. "Put some damn clothes on right now and *then* we can talk."

I wanted to argue. I wanted to scream. I wanted to punch him in the face. But, I did none of that. I stomped to the women's locker room…and got dressed.

We made a pit stop past Jeffrey's dorm before Dr. Rudd's office so he could get a change of clothes. I was sure he regretted forcing a hug once he stepped outside in the brisk January weather.

"Are you sure I can come inside?" I asked while Jeffrey swiped his key pass into the Elijah Cummings pre-honors dormitory.

"Of course," he reassured me. I followed closely behind him through the plain foyer of his dorm. "There's no one here. If Mr. Perry was here there's no way you'd get in. If you think Mrs. Potts is bad, Mr. Perry doesn't miss a thing." I couldn't imagine anyone worse than Mrs. Potts.

Jeffrey's dorm was the total opposite of mine. When I walked inside of my dorm I always felt an overwhelming sense of home. There was always a fire in the fireplace and soft music playing in the foyer. Jeffrey's dorm, however, was cold. It felt like a prison. Besides one plaque in the foyer, listing the names of all the men who stayed in this dorm since 1965, there were no other pictures hanging on the white washed walls. The empty halls made our footsteps echo.

Several couches, with permanent dents in the cushions, sat beneath an enormous flat screen mounted on the wall with wires protruding from it, connecting to several different gaming systems.

He and I filed on to the cramped elevator. He jammed the button for the third floor and it lurched to life with a start.

"Why are you so far from me?" He held his arms out as if I would magically float into them. I wanted to. But, I made myself stay put.

"You're off limits, remember?"

He rolled his eyes. "Not this again." The elevator bobbed on the third floor and the doors sidled open. "This is me," he announced. I followed him until he came to a stop at a set of French doors.

"I'll wait out here," I reported as he slid his key in the lock. The doors swung open to a living room much like the one Regina and I shared.

"At least wait in the living room," he interjected. "I'll only be a second."

I reluctantly followed him inside taking a seat on his plush couch. I couldn't decide if his muted gray walls, which intentionally matched the couch, were ugly or not. I couldn't take my eyes off of it. The pale yellow throw pillows matched a bowl full of lemons on the side table and it all fit perfectly together, weirdly.

"Did you decorate?" I leaned over, fingering a lemon.

He appeared back in the living room shirtless and I clenched my legs closed, ignoring the throbbing that began. I tried to keep my eyes focused on his and not let them travel to his chiseled chest. And I tried not to imagine what treasure I'd find if I unzipped the pants that hung loosely off his waist.

"Hell no." He laughed. I watched his abs contract, taunting me because I couldn't touch them. "Brandon did all of this.

That guy is like the black Martha Stewart," he joked, retreating back into his room.

I took a deep breath when he was finally out of my sight. I had to get myself together. I hadn't seen Jeffrey in about five weeks. I didn't know whether I was feeling happy or sad, anxious or calm. All of our memories flooded back to me. My emotions changed with the passing moments, like every time I saw him smile or the way he stroked his goatee when he was searching for the right words to say. I fanned my overheated face with one of the pillows.

Jeffrey was not mine. He could never be mine, I chanted inside my head. Then why was he so fine? He appeared in the doorway again, fully dressed, unfortunately.

"Oh, no bow tie," I noticed his naked neck. He pulled on his Calvin Kline trench coat and knotted it at the waist.

"I don't wear one every day. Do I?"

"You wear one every time I see you. Well, except those few days during finals." I nudged him in the ribs, smiling, anything to finally give into the urges to touch him. He didn't return the expression. His eyes grew cold and unforgiving. I knew I hit a sensitive subject, shutting down all possibilities of our bodies colliding again.

"Do you want to look at these grades, or what?" He punched the button for the lobby and we shakily descended downwards.

"Yeah," I answered, careful not to say anything more until we reached Dr. Rudd's office.

The Student Services building, much like Jeff's dorm, and the rest of the campus, was empty. It was so dark inside, we could barely see in front of our hands. We felt our way through the building. I held on to the tail of his coat until we reached a stairwell.

"So this can't be a part of your job description if we have to sneak around," I pointed out as he and I ascended the dank stairwell.

"Well, it's not necessarily a part of my job *description*," he admitted. We reached the second floor and, after a few feet, found ourselves at Dr. Rudd's locked office. Jeffrey must have felt the irritation emanating out of my pores.

"I have a key," he told me, digging into his pocket. I whipped out my cell phone and turned on my flashlight app revealing at least ten keys crowding one ring.

"How do you know which one it is?" I asked.

"I don't." His eyes guiltily met mine. "His door is usually unlocked. I figured we could walk right in."

"I bet you all those times you walked right in are during the semester," I countered sarcastically, patting him on the shoulder.

"Whatever." He laughed. "Just hold the light still."

We went through about four or five tries before he slid a key into the lock with ease. I held my breath and the door clicked open.

"That didn't take long," he said happily, walking inside the office. He flicked on the lights and headed over to Dr. Rudd's computer.

I slapped the lights off. "We're not supposed to be in here! Are you crazy?" My eyes adjusted to the darkness again.

"His office faces the back of the campus; no one is going to see us."

"I don't want to chance it." I joined him at Dr. Rudd's desk. Jeffrey lifted the laptop screen and it immediately asked for a password.

"Don't tell me you don't know that either." I rolled my eyes in the dark. Only the glow of the laptop surrounded us.

"It's always the same set of numbers. Sometimes it's backwards or forwards. It may be scrambled up, but always the same numbers."

Jeffrey slowly punched four numbers into the bar and it opened on the first try. I tried to act like I wasn't looking at him when he gave me the 'I told you so' grin. He clicked around on the desktop until he found the school roster. He pulled it up and scrolled until he found my name.

"Raevyn E. Jones," he whispered. "Cumulative GPA 3.3."

"You've got to be kidding me!" I pushed him out of the chair. I wanted to see it for myself. Jeffrey dropped to the ground with a thud. I ran my finger across the screen and Jeffrey was right. Carmichael gave me a B minus making my GPA just shy of the pre-honors qualifications.

"He knew I needed a 3.5. He did this on purpose!" I kicked Dr. Rudd's desk.

"What am I going to do? They are going to kick me out!" I rattled off all the things that were running around in my mind. Miss Tanner, Regina, and Andrea would get what they wanted. Once the grades were finalized, I would be out of B. W. Fitz and back in Maryland.

I knew I shouldn't have written that paper for the final. I should have went along with his elitist theory and secured myself a passing grade. I wanted to kick myself in the ass for trying to be different. Now, I was doomed.

Jeffrey pulled himself off the floor. "Calm down. Maybe I can go talk to him before the students get back. I'll be civilized and I can ask him nicely."

"There's no negotiation with Carmichael. It's that damn Miss Tanner—" I stopped my rant in its tracks and a mischievous thought dropped into my mind. "Can't you just…change it?"

"You want me to lose my job?" Jeffrey stumbled over his words as he explained, "It's done. The semester is over. I…I can't."

"You can just change it right now and we can get out of here," I offered. "Or we can keep strategizing on ways to get Carmichael to change my grade. You and I both know that won't happen." I crossed my arms over my chest in protest, hoping he'd give into my ways.

Jeffrey looked around the room nervously like there were hidden cameras in the walls. "Wouldn't he notice?" His voice spiked.

"You said yourself that Dr. Rudd is so oblivious. He's had the same password for years, right?"

Jeffrey nodded like he was considering it. "Carmichael will surely notice his grade was changed. Especially if he gave you a B just so you could get kicked out."

"I don't care. I just need a 3.5. I can't go home." I placed my head in my hands. If I went home my father would kill me. This was his last ditch resort and I blew it. Why couldn't I do anything right for a change?

"You can still be a student here. You just won't be in the program."

"You don't understand," I mumbled. A few moments passed between us and I knew Jeffrey could feel my desperation. "I – I just… I can't go home."

I was thankful he couldn't see my face right now because for the first time I was on the brink of tears. Just a few months ago I wanted anything to be home with Antoine and now I was crying to stay. Jeffrey's fingers tapped a few keys.

"Raevyn Jones, 3.5," Jeffrey announced.

I looked over his shoulder and he made my cumulative GPA a 3.5 on the dot. "How many times have you done this?"

He looked up at me. "I haven't."

"Okay, let's go," I said before my morals kicked in and I changed my mind. I worked really hard this semester, harder than I have ever worked before. I deserved that GPA. Miss Tanner and Carmichael would know it too when I showed up next semester. I proved that a girl from a rinky-dink community college could take *and* pass pre-honors classes at B. W. Fitz. I deserved to be here.

I pulled Dr. Rudd's door open as Jeffrey closed out the program and shut his computer down again. The green glow of the laptop dimmed out and I felt Jeffrey slide his hand into mine when we bolted down the hallway. We dashed down the stairs together and I tried to hold back my giddy laughter when we finally reached the courtyard outside.

"You're officially a pre-honors student for the spring semester, Miss Jones."

I flung my arms around his neck. "Thank you, Jeffrey," I squealed. "You saved me!"

He wrapped his arms around my waist and pulled me off the ground easily. I braced my hands on his athletic shoulders. There were moments during the Christmas break where I longed to have Jeffrey in my presence, let alone touching me. I relished in the moment, and let myself relax into his embrace.

"Anything for you," he whispered, cupping his hands under me. I didn't even bother to swat them away. He lowered my body onto his, slowly, sensually so we were face to face. I could

168 | Necole Ryse

feel his heartbeat quicken under his coat when I wrapped my legs around his frame.

My body felt like I had just swallowed fire. With Jeffrey, I always felt like I could internally combust at any second when his hands were on me, something I never felt with Antoine.

"I couldn't imagine being at Fitz without you." He brought his face closer and closer to mine and then his full lips brushed mine gently. I opened my mouth, allowing his tongue to explore.

A branch snapped near us and Jeffrey let go of me. I gained my balance before I dropped to the concrete and we spun around in the opposite direction. A bush rustled nearby as if someone stood there, watching us.

I could have been the heat of the moment, or that I was imagining things, but for a split second, I thought I smelled Chanel No. 5.

Faculty began to trickle in, one by one, and eventually the campus came back into school mode. Instead of quiet lunch or dinner dates between Jeffrey and I, which I imagined would be extra special and romantic, we rarely got to see each other. I wanted more than anything to see him for more than a few minutes a day in passing when he would go to the Student Services building or when I would go to the gym.

After what happened that night outside of Dr. Rudd's office, he decided that we shouldn't see each other again, at least not until the semester officially began. Final grades had been posted and I received my schedule for spring semester without any problems, not even an email from Miss Tanner. But still, Jeffrey didn't want to take any chances in case we were seen that night. It seemed like every time we got close, there was something else that pulled us apart again. Just thinking about it made me irritated and I was actually looking forward to burying myself in work. At least if I was bogged down with projects and papers I wouldn't have had any time to think of Jeffrey.

As much as I wanted to remember every moment he and I shared, I knew I needed to forget them. So, I ran anytime I thought about Jeffrey.

It took my mind off of everything. It drowned out all the noise in my life, the thoughts, the fears, the apprehension—until there was nothing left.

Nothing but silence and the constant pat of my sneakers against the sidewalk.

The sun had long since retired behind the clouds when I got the urge to run. I spent hours stalking Jeffrey's Facebook page, drooling at his shirtless Turks and Caicos pictures, when I saw one with Regina on his back. Her long, sculpted legs were wrapped around his waist, and the two of them were smiling at each other as if they knew they would spend the rest of their lives like that, on resorts and islands.

I slammed my laptop shut and realized I needed a release. Bad.

I jammed my feet in my running shoes and judging by the fire coursing through my veins, I needed a long, exhausting run to get Jeffrey off my mind. I snatched Regina's iPod off the mantle. Since she liked encroaching on other people's property I figured I would return the favor.

I took off toward the east side of campus. A hopeful part of me wished I'd run into Headmaster but I knew that wouldn't happen. With the wind out of my sails, a lazy bone kicked in and I decided to cut through the woods instead of following the trail around the lake. I'd be done in half the time, and judging from the sky, snow would fall soon.

Moonlight sliced through the tops of the trees and shattered like glass on the forest floor, only lighting some of my way. The rugged terrain gave my calves and thighs the ultimate workout. And just when I thought about turning back, I dipped beneath a low hanging branch (that was sure to behead me if I hadn't acted so quickly) and my foot caught something, clipping the toe of my shoe. Before I could brace myself, I toppled forward, slamming on the cold ground, face first.

My headphones popped out of my ears and something skittered away. Stars exploded behind my eyes and when I finally got myself together to get up, I realized I was inches away from the lake. Regina's iPod skated across the lake's frozen surface, too far from my reach.

"Fuck!" I kicked a dead tree trunk next to me. My feet sank deeper into the sodden earth as it topped over drunkenly. *How the hell am I going to get her iPod back?* I picked up a stray branch and swung it out to the lake. It clipped the device, sending it spinning in the opposite direction. I realized, reluctantly, that there was only one way to get it back.

I cursed under my breath, calling that iPod everything but its right name. I tried to convince myself that there were a million other ways to get it back without having to venture on the ice. All roads led back to the obvious. I bounced on my toes and shook out my nervous hands. I decided to just do it.

I leaned forward, stepping on the ice with one foot. Gradually, carefully. I refused to breathe. *You're light as a feather,* I thought, as I lifted my other foot onto the ice. I winced, convinced it would cave under my weight, but nothing happened. I took another hesitant step and then another until I was standing on top of the iPod. I kicked it back toward the bank and turned around when I saw someone standing there.

Watching.

I froze, too scared to move. Heavy puffs of smoke expelled from the person's lungs. I watched it dissipate into the air. The person was dressed head to toe in black. A ski mask covered most of his or her face.

B?

And just when I thought things couldn't possibly get any worse, they did. B grabbed the dead tree trunk and chucked it directly at me.

"No!" I heard my scream echo and a maniacal laugh swallowed it whole. The trunk slammed at my feet but it didn't break the surface. I was too horrified to move, that was, until the surface finally cracked.

Weight shifted under me. My legs floated apart and water slipped into my shoes. I knew if I didn't do something I would drown. Visions of my bloated, frozen, and decomposed body flashed through my mind and I slipped into action. Chunks of ice separated from one another in ear-splitting cracks. Water spread over the surface, gobbling up everything solid around me, flooding toward me, drunk with my imminent death. I leapt to my right and my foot missed the surface. I clawed at the surface, pulling myself up.

B followed me, launching logs right at my face. Dirt stung my eyes and I scrambled toward the bank. B sprinted away when I got close, disappearing within the woods. I grabbed Regina's iPod with one motion when I felt the ice break away completely.

Blistering cold water pierced my skin like a million needles all at once, stabbing my heart with shock. My mouth filled with muddy water. My heartbeat grew erratic. With numb fingers, I banged on the surface, kicking until I found another opening. I coughed up the filthy lake water, sucking in air at the same time. On pure adrenaline, I pulled myself from the lake.

January air assaulted me as I thrashed through the woods and back toward campus. I couldn't feel anything until I slammed chest first into someone. I stumbled backwards.

"S-sorry." My teeth clanged against each other. Somewhere an owl hooted. The street lamps were a threatening yellow. My legs quaked.

"I was hoping I'd run into you," someone said. "I didn't think it'd be literal."

The edges of my vision blurred. The sidewalk uncorked from the earth and ran into me.

A sickening mixture of bleach and chocolate brought me hurtling back through a tunnel of darkness. My eyes burned and I was really, really cold.

"Rae?" I heard the curve of Andre's voice. My skin made a nauseating slurp sound when I pulled myself off the table from where I'd been drooling. I swiped at my mouth when he pushed a steaming cup of hot chocolate toward me. I reached for it hungrily. A quiet cough introduced Brandon who was standing in the corner, clutching a book to his chest.

"Are you okay, Raevyn?" Brandon asked. Dre's fingers crept over and stroked mine.

"What are you doing here?" The smoky smell of burning wood warmed me. I was home. Where was Mrs. Potts? I couldn't imagine her letting two boys in the foyer without her supervision. I glanced over my shoulder. Maybe she was watching out of view.

"You fainted and I think you hit your head." Dre looked over at Brandon. "I didn't know who else to call. I figured you would know what to do since you always be studying that book." He nodded at Brandon's trusty Anatomy book.

"I thought something was wrong with Corrine." Brandon crossed the room.

"Sorry if I woke you up. I'm Andre Mason." Dre extended his hand and Brandon shook it.

"Brandon Delaney. How'd you get my number?"

"Her phone." Andre pointed at the muddy mess on the table.

"Let me see." Brandon dropped down in a seat across from me. He waved his finger between my eyes. "What are you feeling?"

"Cold," I answered, concentrating on his finger—or fingers—I couldn't tell.

"What happened tonight, Rae?"

"Regina's iPod fell." I pulled the waterlogged thing from my pocket. "I saved it." He looked over at Dre who shrugged. "She needs to go to the hospital. She might have a concussion. Did she say anything?"

"Nah." Dre tugged on one of his locks. "I ran into her and she just fainted."

"Her clothes are soaking wet. Are you sure that's all that happened?"

"Man, you know everything I do," he replied in a panicked voice.

"She needs to get warm. I think we'll have to wake up Mrs. Potts, man. She might get hypothermia."

"Alright," Dre conceded. "I'll wait here with her." He draped his coat over my shoulder and pushed my chair in front of the fireplace.

"No." I finally found my voice. "I'm fine." I jumped up and the room folded in on itself. I sat down again.

"Rae, you need medical attention," Brandon said, steadily moving towards Mrs. Potts' room.

"I need to go to bed, that's all."

His shoulders slumped and he looked to Dre for backup, but again, he shrugged. "Let's just get her in bed and we can deal with it in the morning. It's past midnight."

"Raevyn, are you sure you're okay?" Brandon sat back down beside me.

"Yes." I nodded.

He planted a kiss on my forehead. "I will check on you first thing in the morning."

"Brandon?" He turned while shrugging on his pea coat.

"Please don't tell Jeffrey about this." He opened his mouth, debating on arguing before agreeing.

"Fine. Text me when she's asleep," Brandon said to Dre. A cold blast of air swept through the foyer when he left.

"Let's get you upstairs." Andre scooped me into his arms like I weighed absolutely nothing. He grunted. "You're heavier than you look," he joked while we boarded the elevator. I buried my face in his shirt. He smelled like Antoine.

"It's the wet clothes," I mumbled.

"Right," he chuckled.

I rummaged through my drawers and found a pair of pajamas. I stripped my wet clothes off, dropping them into my trashcan. Dre waited patiently outside my room, pacing back and forth, consulting his watch every few seconds and looking back at my bedroom door.

"I'm fine," I called out to him. I wasn't. I could barely stand long enough to get my arms through my shirt. I climbed into bed the second he busted through the door.

"Sorry," he blushed when he saw me flip the covers over my exposed thighs. "You were just too quiet. I couldn't wait any longer."

"It's okay."

I realized I never had a boy within the walls of my room. He backed up against the door as if he was invading my personal space.

"I, uh, been thinking a lot since that night." He dug his hand in his jeans pocket.

"The ball?" I hugged a pillow to my chest.

He nodded. "I don't really know what else to say besides I'm not scared anymore."

"Scared?" I echoed.

"Of what people would say when they found out."

"Found out that you're a Mason?" I asked, feeling sleep creep into the recesses of my mind. My eyes drooped while he spoke.

"That I'm not a Mason." He dragged the toe of his boot in my carpet.

"What?"

"I was adopted when I was an infant. My parents decided to tell me the summer before college. Imagine my shock when I found out my parents weren't really my parents and my siblings weren't really my brother and sister. I wasn't *really* a Mason." He sighed deeply like he was pushing the memory out of his mind. He stared down at his fingers while he talked.

"Long story short I found my biological parents, the Mouton's, from New Orleans. I learned French and I decided to start my own legacy. I declined my full ride to Morehouse and got into Fitz on scholarship. I was proud of that until I saw you that night at the party."

"Andre…" I reached out to him, but no words came. "I'm so sorry."

"Don't you ever be sorry." He was silent for a while before he finally said, "Raevyn Jones, you saved me."

Somewhere between Dre leaving and sleep conquering me, my phone buzzed.

I groggily swiped the screen and the text message read: **I could have killed you. Make it easy on yourself and take the hint before it's too late -B**

Paranoid wasn't exactly the best word I would use to describe how I felt over the next couple of days. I crept around corners, and jumped at every unfamiliar sound. I refused to drink tap water for fear it would taste like mud. I couldn't even look at the other side of Fitz. Whoever B was, he or she did a great job of scaring the hell out of me that night. After my throbbing, debilitating headache died down, and after answering each one of Brandon's unlicensed health concerns, I finally returned to real life.

Coming that close to death wasn't exactly what I thought would take place at Fitz. I considered taking B's advice and leaving, but I had no place else to go. But, if I stayed any longer, I could die.

A black town car swept the driveway of the South gate and before the driver could get out to open the door for me, I jumped inside. I didn't want to spend more time than necessary out in the open. With Andrea gone, my days of luxury limo rides were over and until I found out who B was and what he or she wanted, I was prey.

"Where to?" a short Italian man asked. His eyes smiled at me in the rear view mirror.

"Downtown, um, Vincent's please," I answered, slinking back in my seat. My body jostled as we drove over the familiar cobblestone streets. The knots in my stomach loosened when I recognized the bustling city streets of Ohio.

Tomorrow was the official start of the semester, which meant in a few hours my roommate and her friends would return. I was dreading this moment since they left for Turks and Caicos. I didn't know how Regina would act towards me or if she was so sun-kissed and relaxed that she forgot about the whole ordeal, and coincidentally forget her ruined iPod.

Something told me she wouldn't forget. Girls like Regina never forget. I hoped that by the time I got back from downtown I'd have a few hours to myself before she and her posse returned.

I scanned the street and my eyes landed hungrily on a bright red Ferrari 458 Spider convertible—Antoine's dream car. For as long as I'd known him, he wanted it. My heart dropped to my stomach. *Was he out? Was he coming to get me?* I knew it was a silly idea but I had to see if he was inside.

I quickly paid the driver and hopped out of the cab. I raced down the street and blasted through an elderly couple. The crotchety wife squealed when her Saks Fifth Ave bag dropped to the concrete with a crunch. I politely handed it back to her, apologizing profusely, but she still managed to muster enough strength in her old bones to call me everything but a child of God.

I ran a few more steps and directly into the arms of another stranger. Our legs tangled, but I didn't take my eyes off the car. I peered into the tinted windows, and couldn't see who, if anyone, was inside. A small part—okay, a very large part—of me wanted it to be Antoine.

"Whoa."

The familiar scent of the stranger tantalized my senses. Jeffrey gripped me by the shoulders.

"What's your deal? You practically clotheslined that old lady back there." He laughed, trying to steady my squirming body. I tried to glance around him, through him, over him at the car's windows but there was no one inside.

Jeffrey's eyes followed mine to the Ferrari. "It's just a Spider." He shrugged.

"I just thought I knew who…" I swallowed, catching my breath. I had to tell myself this wasn't Antoine. He wasn't coming. He wasn't out. "I just thought I knew whose car that was."

"You do." He smiled. "It's mine." He pressed a button on his remote and the lights blinked at us. "Got it a few years ago for my birthday," he explained.

Just then, a Dodge Charger with blacked out windows whipped around the corner. I could hear the bass thumping through his sub-woofers. The whole street vibrated along to the beat. People slowed down and stared, trying to figure out why shop windows were trembling. Their eyes traveled over to the car in the middle of the street pumping out an explicit hip-hop song. A slow-burning angry fire spread through my body.

"Got dammit, Wade," I cursed under my breath. Wade spotted me and got out of his car, which was parked in the middle of the street.

Literally, the middle of the goddamned street.

I'd gotten so sidetracked by the Ferrari that I forgot about our drop off. Several cars laid on their horns when they saw he wasn't moving anymore. He flipped off the line of cars and waved at me to cross the street. His burly demeanor, coupled with his obnoxious behavior, screamed threatening. I was about to move towards him when Jeffrey blocked my path.

"You know that guy?" He looked curiously between Wade and me.

Wade incessantly waved. "Yo, Bird!" he screamed.

Bird as in raven.

Raevyn as in me.

My face burned. Why did he have to call me that in front of Jeffrey?

"Bird!" he screamed louder as if the traffic and his music would stop me from hearing him. He beckoned me over. "What you doin'? Come 'ere!"

Cars zoomed past him angrily. Someone must have reported the commotion because before long a patrol car sidled alongside him. Two officers hopped out, analyzing him before walking over, their hands hovering over their weapons.

"Oh, God," I whispered. I prayed I didn't have to witness Wade get arrested, or worse, die. I didn't have enough money for two criminals or a funeral.

While he argued with the officer, he gestured wildly toward me, waving me over again. I couldn't go over there, especially with Jeffrey standing here. It would only be a matter of time before it got to Regina and Andrea that I met some hoodlum and gave him a roll of cash. Before long, I would be a drug dealer. And then I'd be on the first thing smoking back to Maryland.

"No," I answered Jeffrey, who eyed Wade like he was a common dog with a bad case of fleas.

"Then let's go," he advised, leading me to his car as if Wade would shoot us both. The butterfly doors shot up in the air, welcoming us.

"Yo, Bird! What the fuck?" I heard Wade call one last time before I slid inside of Jeff's car.

He sped off, leaving Wade behind. I could only see the whir of blue and red lights when Jeffrey turned the corner. I dropped my head into my hands. Wade was going to kill me. Antoine would revive me and then kill me again. I was sure of it.

"You okay?" Jeffrey asked, pulling into a covering. An acne-ridden kid rushed over in a red vest. It read: VALET. His eyes almost fell out of his head and he practically slobbered the entire time Jeffrey was giving him instructions on what to do with his car. He nodded blindly.

"Yeah, sure man."

"I'm fine. That music gave me a headache," I lied, pretending to massage my temples.

"I have something that will fix that." Jeffrey gestured to the building he and I were walking into. The smell of tortillas and salsa danced around my nostrils teasingly. How did Jeffrey know Mexican food was my favorite?

"This place has the best Mexican food on the planet." Jeffrey placed his hand on the small of my back as we walked in together.

He shook hands with the host, an older Caucasian man who seemed ecstatic to see him. They made small talk about each other's families (I thought I heard him ask about Regina) as we journeyed through the carpeted restaurant. We skirted around tables and passed a private room where a live mariachi band was playing for a birthday. A woman in a sombrero danced in five-inch heels with maracas to the beat. He led us to a private booth in the back of the restaurant.

"Enjoy, Mr. Donnelly." The host nodded to Jeffrey and placed two menus in front of us. A server passed us with a margarita the size of my head.

"Want one?" Jeffrey asked, following my eyes. "They are really good here."

"Jeffrey, you're nineteen," I lowered my voice. I should have known age didn't matter. It only mattered if you had the money to pay for it.

He cut his eyes at me as if he could read my mind. He sucked his teeth, throwing his hand in the air and a server rushed over. Her hair was disheveled and she was packing some serious luggage under her eyes. The concealer she smeared on that morning must have rubbed off with the lunch crowd. She probably wasn't aware of how tired she looked. I knew the feeling.

"We'll take two strawberry…" Jeffrey looked over at me to confirm the flavor. I didn't care if it was dirt flavored. I could order drinks from an actual restaurant without getting carded? Rich people had it made. I nodded and he repeated, "Strawberry margaritas, please."

"Right away." She smiled politely and scampered away, scribbling on her overrun notepad, nearly careening into a bus boy.

"See? Easy," he said as if this was normal behavior. Of course it was normal for him. Even after months at B. W. Fitz the things these people could get away with still shocked me.

"We can't do that where I'm from." I pulled up the menu and scanned the options. Everything was in Spanish. My extent of Spanish was learned from the Chihuahua on the Taco Bell commercials or Dora the Explorer. In fact, my extent of

Mexican food was Taco Bell. They didn't have crunch wraps here? *How do you say 'crunch wrap' in Spanish?*

The waitress came back and placed two margaritas in front of us. I immediately slid my straw in the frozen beauty and took a long sip. I grimaced from the brain freeze. Jeffrey tried not to spew margarita everywhere when he laughed.

"You're so cute," he said, flashing his smile at me. How could he manage to make me go weak at the knees while I was sitting down?

"Thanks?" I responded.

"Tell me about Atlanta," he started, pushing his margarita aside and knitting his fingers together over his menu. "You guys do things so differently. You dress like hell, no cell phone, no margaritas."

"That's just me," I cut him off before he got carried away. "I was raised differently. My dad was really strict with me." That wasn't a lie. "I was kept on a really tight leash."

"Total opposite for me." Jeffrey took another sip of his margarita and rolled his eyes. "My parents gave me anything I wanted. Sometimes I wished I was kept on a tight leash."

"Why? You guys have it all." I pointed to the drink.

"Money, yeah." He shook his head. "But, I can't tell you the last time I saw my mom and dad together in the same room." He thought for a second. "Maybe my high school graduation? Even then Dad was working. He couldn't take one day off."

My heart panged. I couldn't imagine not having parents. The thought of it sounded nice for a second, but I really don't know where I'd have been without my father. I certainly wouldn't have been here, sipping margaritas with Jeffrey, that's for sure. Being wealthy came with a hefty price tag. You work so hard to get money and then you have to work even harder to keep it. I wondered how many nights Jeffrey went to bed without a goodnight kiss, or someone to yell at him for coming in the house after midnight. Never, I guessed.

"What does your dad do?"

"Lawyer." He twisted the cloth napkin around his finger. "You know those celebrity scandals where some douche is busted with a kilo of cocaine but only serves like three days in jail? Yeah, that's my dad. He's the big time."

Whoa. "And your mom?" I asked.

"OB/GYN," he rattled off like he'd been telling people this all of his life.

"Does that bother you?" I asked, taking another big gulp of margarita. I felt my cell phone buzz. I pulled it out of my purse. I had three missed calls from Wade.

Oh shit.

"It used to when I was a kid," he admitted. "You want your parents to be at the spelling bees and football games but I got used to it. None of my friends' parents were there either. That's just the way it goes." He shrugged.

"That's why you were surprised when I came to Fitz?" I realized. "Because my dad was there?"

"I'd never seen anything like it. And you only had *one* bag," he exclaimed.

"I've never been one to put much stock in *things*." It was mostly because I didn't have any money to buy nice things. Even when Regina and Andrea swiped their debit cards freely for me I would always grimace at the price of things. I knew that even if I were 'black excellence' I'd still be most comfortable in my graffiti Levi's.

"So what are you supposed to do? Be a mortician like Brandon? Or are you more of a funeral director? Counsel the grieving families? Or an undertaker? I see those guns, Rae. You been burying folks over the break?"

"What?" I shifted in my seat. Suddenly, the booth felt like I was sitting on a bed of rocks.

"When Corrine and I graduate we're going to law school like our dads. Regina will probably take a position at the school like her mom. Andrea will probably work with the label and Brandon is more than likely going to be a mortician. What's your plan?"

Construction? "I don't want to do what my dad does," I said under my breath. I really hadn't given much thought to life after graduation. I just wanted to make it through the semester alive.

Jeffrey scoffed. "Tell me about it." He ran his hands over the back of his neck.

I switched the heat off me. "What would you do if you could do anything in the world?"

Jeffrey looked up at me and smiled embarrassingly. "I – I can't be anything in the world so, this is just a dumb question." He waved the question away as if it were a gnat at a barbecue.

"What if I told you that you could?" He shook his head at me as if I was asking him to convert to Scientology. "You can do whatever you want to do. You can make your own legacy."

"I'd be a race car driver," Jeffrey mumbled.

"That's awesome." I smiled.

His eyes lit up at my reaction but dimmed instantly. "Regina and the rest of my family think it's stupid. But if there were no legacies, Regina would want to dance. Her idea is just as farfetched as mine. I just love that feeling when I drive fast."

Jeffrey closed his eyes and imitated being behind a wheel. "The closest I'll ever get to that is that Spider out there." He nodded toward the parking lot.

I remembered Regina's tattoo. I wondered if her parents knew about her audition. Time stretched between us when he asked, "What would you do?"

I shrugged. "I don't know. But it won't be in my legacy." I couldn't imagine seeing myself in a hard hat and I shuddered at the thought of dead bodies.

"You *really* don't want to be in your legacy?" He squinted his eyes at me as if I was delusional. "Everyone follows their legacy."

I was committing a cardinal sin. This whole legacy thing was engrained in them since birth. I felt horrible that they couldn't make their own decisions about their future. Their careers and even their spouses were pre-determined. It was almost criminal that they weren't in control of their own destiny.

"Maybe I'm just the exception, not the rule."

"You've proved that, Raevyn Jones, time and time again." When he rose from his seat and leaned over the table, bringing his handsome face close, I couldn't help but allow myself to fall into him. Maybe it was the tequila that had gone straight to my brain. It didn't matter. All that mattered right now was Jeffrey.

I silenced Wade's fifth call, and in the middle of a Mexican restaurant, that wasn't Taco Bell, I made out with Jeffrey Vincent Eugene Donnelly the fourth. Regina's Jack.

He parked his Ferrari amidst the BMW's and Aston Martin's in the staff parking lot. I spotted Corrine lugging her pink leopard print Jessica Simpson suitcase up the steps of our dormitory and I knew Regina and Andrea couldn't be too far behind.

"I'd better go," I said dejectedly, nodding my head in her direction. Jeffrey planted a sweet, elongated kiss on my lips.

"See you at dinner?"

My fingers lingered in his before I finally pulled away.

"Wouldn't miss it," I replied.

And like that, he and I went our separate ways, back to pretending that we didn't exist to each other.

I walked into a shit storm when I opened the door to my room. Corrine and Regina were digging through their suitcases and talking so quickly it seemed like they were speaking a different language.

Corrine's skin was a beautiful bronze color. The island sun did wonders for her complexion. Andrea didn't look up when I walked in. She dug her hand into the box of Cheez-It's and chewed, while flicking channels on the TV.

"I had them before I left," Regina cried. "My grandma gave those earrings to me." She threw a Tori Burch sandal over her shoulder. It landed at my feet. Corrine joined in ripping her suitcase apart.

"They have to be in here somewhere," Corrine said in the most reassuring tone, picking up the clothes Regina had thrown haphazardly, and folded the items neatly on the sofa. "When's the last time you saw them?"

"I don't know!" Regina said in an irritated voice. "I know I had them before we left." She flopped down in the mouth of her suitcase bringing a chiffon dress to her eyes. "How could I have been so careless?" She sobbed nastily, wiping her nose on the garment.

"No, no." Corrine tried to reach for the dress that now had a huge wet stain on the front of it. "Not the Versace." She grabbed the end of it and Regina slapped her hand away.

This scene had gone on too long.

I snatched the box of Kleenex off the mantle.

"Here." I offered to Regina. She looked up at me like a kid who was lost in a mall and I was a security guard, her savior.

"Thanks, Rae." She traded the tissues for the dress.

Corrine shook it out and assured her, "We can get this cleaned. Don't you worry about it." She slipped a hanger through the shoulders of the dress and hung it on Regina's door.

"You're the only one worried." Andrea paused on a Lifetime movie, and then switched the channel again.

"I'm trying to be positive here," Corrine countered. "At least I'm helping her." She snapped her hand on her hip, staring down the back of Andrea's head.

"She said she didn't have them on the trip. We're wasting time looking for them in the suitcase." She flipped around on the couch facing me. "Tell them it's stupid, Raevyn. No one listens to me. I'm the *bitch*," Andrea mumbled and turned toward the TV again.

Well, that part was true.

I realized they obviously weren't mad at me anymore. Or maybe they were too preoccupied to give a damn. Maybe Corrine was right.

"What are you guys looking for?" I asked, reaching down for Regina. I pulled her out of her suitcase. Her leg had a huge, painful red imprint where the handle pressed on her calf.

"Regina's earrings," Corrine volunteered.

"They're more than just earrings!" Regina screamed. "Don't say it like they're some piece of shit from *Macy's*. My grandma gave them to me. They're special!"

Corrine threw her hands up in surrender.

"What do they look like?" I scanned the floor as if they would magically appear. "Maybe I can help."

"We've been looking all morning." Andrea sank down in the couch. "They aren't here."

"They're Chanel." Regina sniffed. Her nose was stuffed from all the crying she'd done and now she sounded like Chuckie Finster.

"*Original* Chanel," she emphasized with a neck swivel. "They were my grandmothers. She gave them to my mother when she turned seventeen. I've had them since I was seventeen. I'm supposed to give them to my daughter when she turns seventeen, but I lost them." She slapped her hands onto her legs like a five-year-old. "I lost them," she whimpered.

Bile jumped up my throat. I silenced the alarms that were blaring in my head.

Chanel earrings.

The pool drain.

Wade.

"We've torn this place upside down." Corrine plopped on the couch with Andrea and let out a tired sigh. "They aren't here, Reggie."

Regina's lip quivered when she looked over at me. The prissy princess who applied anti-wrinkle cream religiously every night, and wouldn't dare show her face without mascara, didn't even care that her eyes were swollen and that she was less than presentable. Seeing Regina in such a wreck made me want to curl into a ball and cry like a baby too.

"Can you look around for them?" Regina pulled her fingers apart, just hardly. "They're small studs."

I nodded, feeling sick. "Of course."

Regina sobbed for at least another hour. I was so mad I could have punched myself in the face. I knew they were expensive. I wished I would have known it was a family heirloom. How could I have given her earrings away like that? How could I have done any of it?

I stomped around my room, plucking myself in the forehead, silently screaming until my lungs burned. I was wrong. I shouldn't have agreed to help Antoine. I was holding on to the past when there was nothing there for me anymore. I needed to leave that life behind for good. As much as I hated to admit it, my dad was right and he had been right all along.

From this point forward, I was done with Wade, Antoine, and everything else I left back in Maryland. My future was here at B. W. Fitz, with Jeffrey, and I was going to make it right with Regina, Andrea, and Corrine.

A couple of days later, my cell phone vibrated violently on my desk while I was doing my homework. I swiped the screen without another thought and heard a computerized voice. I accepted the charges and I tried to maintain my composure when I heard Antoine's voice flood over my receiver. I knew exactly what would happen next.

"Bird," he stated plainly. From his voice alone I could tell he was holding something back.

"Antoine," I answered. I sat up straight as if he could see me. I chomped down on the edge of my pen, grinding my teeth over the cap, anticipating his anger.

He can't hurt you, Raevyn, I told myself. I was stronger than this. Antoine made his choices and I made mine. He couldn't hold that over my head anymore.

"Wade told me what happened." He sighed.

"I figured he would."

"He said you were with some rich guy in my Ferrari. Do you want to talk about it?"

"His name is Jeffrey, not some *guy*," I corrected him. "And no, I don't want to talk about it."

"I didn't take you for the type of girl that could be bought." I was about to respond but he continued, "You went up to that school and you changed on me, Bird. Wade told me that you would and I didn't listen to him. I didn't want to listen to him and I guess that was my fault. I thought I knew my girl. I guess I was wrong, huh?"

"Antoine, stop. Just let me explain."

"I asked you if you wanted to talk about it and you refused. You don't get to explain!" His voice shook me to the core. I was stunned, glued to the seat. He'd never, ever, screamed at me before.

"You can't just leave, Bird. You can't just leave me to die in here. I did this for you!"

"I didn't ask you to—"

"You didn't have to *ask* me. I did it because I loved you. You think that Ferrari-driving nigga would do this for you?"

The computerized voice informed the both of us that he only had thirty more seconds to speak.

"I'll be out soon." His breathing became labored. "I told you I'll always be able to find you, little Bird. This ain't over."

He slammed the receiver down before the countdown reached one.

———

The whole world around me moved in slow motion.

The clock on the dash read 6:37 p.m., just before the seatbelt grabbed my throat. I heard Antoine scream for me, his hands flew frantically, trying to gain control of the car, but it was too late. The cash rained around us, catapulting this way and that, blocking his view of the road. The steering wheel jerked demonically like someone else was driving.

We fishtailed then whipped in the opposite direction. Chunks of gravel jumped, popping against the windshield.

Antoine stomped on the brake. Our tires skid across the road, smoke billowed in the air, and then it felt like we were flying.

My stomach rose then dropped, and before I could scream, before I realized what was happening, my mouth collided with the dashboard when the car finally slammed to a stop.

Steam rolled like black clouds and the world just would not. stop. ringing. What the fuck was that ringing? The metallic taste of blood mixed with the overwhelming smell of burned rubber made me nauseated. A white-hot pain shot through my neck and my brain throbbed so violently that I knew it would explode at any second.

The foggy scenery floated into view. I was in an accident. A car accident. Antoine. I was with Antoine. I was alive. Was he alive?

"Pooh," I managed to say. His name lodged in my throat. I couldn't breathe. I reached carefully for the snap that latched the seatbelt onto my neck. I pressed the button and the belt whipped past my face, securing itself back into place.

My fingers found the stitching in the seat beside me, but there was no Antoine. I blinked through the haziness, feeling the milky smoke coat my throat. I wanted to get up. I had to see Antoine, but my legs were pinned under the mangled front end of the car.

"Pooh," I cried again for him but only silence answered back.

"Antoine!" A scream escaped.

"Don't move." I heard him say to me. "I'm going to get you out, Bird."

"I'm stuck," I answered, attempting to maneuver my legs. Something stabbed my knee.

"Bird, don't move," he said again in a foreign voice. His face was bloody and swollen beyond recognition. Blood splattered everywhere like rain while he tried to shift my seat backwards, drenching my white shirt. After one large push, it finally shifted backwards, freeing my legs from the clump of parts that used to be the front end of his Crown Victoria.

"Do you think you can run?" he asked.

A bolt of pain exploded when he tried to stand me upright. "It hurts," I whimpered, afraid my legs were broken.

"Stand up," he ordered. I righted myself, only for a few seconds before hitting the ground hard.

"Bird!" The gravel from the road popped me in the face when he scrambled over. "You've got to get out of here." His voice was panicked, afraid. Antoine wasn't afraid of anything. What happened? "Take this." He shoved something (paper? money?) in the bend of my fingers. "Get a cab and go home."

"I'm not leaving you," I said, too weak to even think about running.

"Bird, go!" he urged, pulling me to my feet.

"What about you? What will you do?" I coughed through the bills that were saturated in blood. My blood? His blood? My mind tried to backtrack but it was blank. What did we do? What happened?

"You have to get out of here, Bird," he said, planting a kiss on my face. "I love you so much," he said over the sound of blaring sirens that were right on top of us.

"Antoine, no." I felt my knees begin to buckle. "I can't leave."

The blue and red lights began to swirl all around us, making his skin a kaleidoscope of lost possibilities.

"Go fly."

The next day I was in a complete daze. I was just a walking body, going through the motions. I laughed when everyone else did at breakfast and I recited all the words to The Dream speech at morning announcements, but my mind was elsewhere, in Maryland.

Antoine's last words still resounded in my mind, chilling my bones. *Did* Jeffrey buy me? Or did he genuinely care for me like he said? Would he do the things that Antoine did for me? My mind backpedaled and I realized that everything Jeffrey did for me involved money. Was I becoming the girl that Andrea told me about my first day here?

"Boyfriends buy diamonds," I mumbled to myself.

"What?" Corrine asked. "Did you say something?"

"Oh, nothing." I smiled back at her concerned face. Her green eyes darted between mine. Suspicion knitted in her brows and I quickly turned my face from hers.

Although Antoine was good enough for me in Maryland, I was a different person in Ohio. I was no longer the naïve girl. I was Raevyn Elizabeth Jones, a legacy. And I deserved a man that was on the same level. I deserved Jeffrey and that, I decided, was the end of it.

The weather was beginning to break. It definitely wasn't springtime, but it was an unseasonably warm day in January and everyone seemed to take full advantage of the warming sunshine. Clips of conversation traveled like bullets through the courtyard when the morning announcements ended. Corrine's cheeks worked overtime on the gum in her mouth while she tried to blow a bubble the size of her head. Just when she got it big enough, Andrea leaned over and popped it with her stiletto nail. We couldn't help but laugh while Corrine picked the gum off her chin.

Then, a few girls in black bomber jackets passed us. They walked together in unison like a biker gang, parting the crowd without saying a word, almost like I saw Regina and Andrea do on several occasions. Who the hell were *they*? Regina and Andrea exchanged hungry glances and scurried away. Corrine promptly rolled her eyes.

"Not again," she whined as we took off behind our friends.

Keeping up with Regina was hard work. She rounded the corner like Mr. Flash when she heard a high-pitched call.

I plugged my fingers in my ears. "What was that?" I looked over at Andrea who seemed to be as intrigued as Regina was. I'd never seen them more interested in anything, well, besides celebrities and cute guys. They were practically slobbering all over themselves.

"Those," Andrea started, out of breath and wide-eyed, "are the Xi's." A crowd swelled around the fifteen girls, all bunched together in matching black jackets. Each one had different number and letter on the sleeve. They laughed together, each girl, touching one another lightly with smiling eyes. Their smiles

198 | Necole Ryse

faded and they simultaneously made the shape of an X over their chest. Their hair wisped playfully in the wind as they prepared themselves for something.

Something huge.

"The what?" I whispered to Andrea's back.

"Please tell me you're joking," she said through tight lips.

Regina spun around facing the both of us, shooting us a look that probably could have sliced us in half. Andrea pretended her lips and finger were a lock and key.

"Later," Andrea mouthed to me. I looked over at Corrine who wasn't interested in the least. She was facing the opposite way from the group, waiting for it to be over. I, however, was too intrigued to look away.

A shorter girl emerged from the group. The others all silently obeyed her commanding presence and as soon as she took center stage a hush fell over the crowd. I recognized the girl from one of my classes, but I couldn't remember which one. I knew I'd seen her before.

I felt myself jump from when she started speaking. Her voice was thunderous, stretching across the campus, sending a chill up my spine. She barreled through the sorority's profound history, their impacts on the B. W. Fitz campus and then out of nowhere, let out another high-pitched caw that emerged from her belly.

Andrea's smile was the size of a doublewide trailer, while Regina was stone-faced and serious. Her lips moved just slightly as she recited the words to the chant the Xi's began.

As the Xi's began to step together their voices angelically meshed to the rhythm of the beat. Their long hair swung in the wind and none of them faltered. Their synchronized stomps and claps were seamless. They were perfect. Once they finished, a huge applause erupted from the mass of students standing around.

I scanned the crowd before it dispersed and could see the adoration that was embedded in the eyes of the girls standing around. The men looked on with a tantalized sense and I then realized that the Xi's were *it*. How could I become one of those girls?

"*You* don't know who the Xi's are?" Regina asked icily, looking me up and down like she no longer recognized me.

My heart jumped into my mouth.

"Of course I do," I said, swallowing my heartbeat. "I was only joking." I laughed through my words.

"Hello? Earth to Regina," Andrea said, waving her hand in front of Regina's face, who hadn't taken her eyes off of me. "Why so serious?"

"The Xi's aren't joking material." She turned her back to both Andrea and I and stomped away. The three of us followed behind her.

"Don't mind her," Andrea whispered, pulling out a compact mirror and applying a coat of hot pink lipstick. Only she could pull off something so bold. "Every woman in Regina's family is a member of the Xi's. They take it really seriously." She puckered her lips and buried the compact in her LV Neverfull bag.

"*Every* woman?" I repeated.

Corrine nodded. "The Xi's were the first on this campus. The Xi's are the best. There is no other sorority to join, at least in Regina's world," Corrine said under her breath.

"I *heard* you," Regina said, just a few paces ahead of us. She turned around so abruptly that I almost slammed into her. I stumbled over my feet when I heard her declare, "There is no other   sorority."

I had Professor Carmichael again for the spring semester. It was clear this man had it out for me. I could finally make my own schedule and chose to take another African American Studies class. I made sure the teacher was not, I repeat, not Professor Carmichael, so imagine my disdain when he sauntered into class fifteen minutes late.

Our original professor got mystifyingly sick this weekend, or so he explained, and he would now be taking over her course. I felt a weight fall over everyone in the room. This was not going to be fun.

"Miss Jones," he called to me after he spotted me pretending to slam my forehead into my textbook. "Please lock the door so we can begin."

I crossed the room to the door and saw a blur of black rounding the corner. A girl flailed her arms in my direction.

"Hey! Don't close it," she screamed.

"Miss Jones," Carmichael sung. "All you have to do is lock the door."

"Someone's coming." I watched the girl barrel down the long concrete hallway.

"Lock the door," he demanded.

"She's right here." I held the door out and Carmichael hopped from behind the desk just as the girl in the black jacket crossed the threshold.

"Thanks," she whispered, completely out of breath. Her hair swirled behind her and I recognized her as the loudmouth Xi girl. She scooted by Professor Carmichael, neglecting to make eye contact with him and took a seat near the back of the room.

He cut his eyes at me. "When I ask you to do something, I expect you to do it."

"Excuse me?" I whipped around. He didn't intimidate me like he did everyone else. I wasn't afraid of a guy who wore blue Speedos. "She was only a few feet away, calm down." I sat down at my desk, ignoring his death stare.

"Please remove yourself from my classroom." He crossed his arms over his black sheer shirt, waiting for me to pack my things. Several gasps echoed across the classroom. I wasted no time removing myself as he asked.

"Miss Parker," Carmichael boomed across the room. "You were late."

"It won't happen again," she responded. Her voice was small. It was as if she was almost afraid to speak up.

"Good," Carmichael nodded. "Now as soon as Miss Jones leaves we can begin." His lips curled in satisfaction when I slung my bag over my shoulder. He slammed the door behind me when I left.

By the time I arrived at dinner that night my antics with Professor Carmichael had spread all over school.

"Tell me everything." Corrine plopped down in her usual seat. She cut into her steaming pork chop while she eyed me.

There was no greeting. She didn't ask me about the rest of my day. No one was worried about the fact that I almost burned my hair out of my scalp this morning because I fell asleep with the curling iron in it. Everyone just wanted to hear about my standoff with Carmichael. Was he *that* scary to everyone? He wasn't threatening at all. Maddening, never threatening.

"There's nothing to tell." I shrugged, digging my fork into her mound of mashed potatoes. Since when did she eat carbs?

"Oh, come on." She moved one seat closer to me and nudged me in the ribs. "There's no one around." She looked over her shoulder. "You can tell me."

"Really," I answered. "There's nothing to tell. I just left, that's it."

"That's not how I heard it," Brandon interrupted, taking Corrine's open seat. "I heard you let Professor Carmichael *have* it." He pushed his glasses up on his nose, flashing his braces at me. Everyone was waiting on some juicy story and all I did was walk out of the guys' class.

"That's not what happened at all," I corrected him. "All I did was hold the door for that girl." I snapped my fingers trying to remember the name of the sorority.

"What girl?" Corrine asked excitedly, looking around the cafeteria. I joined her in the search but I didn't see her anywhere.

"The short girl, you know, the one in that sorority."

Corrine's eyes looked like they would pop out of her head. "Kamilah?"

"I don't know." I shrugged. "Is she the shortest one? You know the loud one we saw the other day." I turned to Corrine waiting for her confirmation. She just stared back at me as if I was a mental patient.

"Yes." Brandon laughed, shaking his head at my cluelessness. "You held the door for Kamilah Renee Parker, president of Xi Nu Lambda, the only sorority on this campus if you let Regina tell it."

"You better not tell Regina about it," Corrine mumbled. "She'll go insane."

"Tell me what?" Regina asked, whipping her legs gracefully around the bench and taking a seat. She had a huge plate of spinach salad and looked over at Corrine's plate disapprovingly. "Tell me that you're eating instant mashed potatoes?" Regina poked at the mound on Corrine's plate, examining the potatoes like it was a science experiment.

"That your girl is best friends with Kamilah Parker." Brandon pointed at me with his fork.

Regina's eyes followed Brandon's fork like there were more than one of me sitting in my seat. "Oh please," she scoffed. "Raevyn?"

I shot her a 'what's that supposed to mean?' look and she backtracked.

"No offense, but when would *you* ever run into Kamilah Parker? You guys don't even run in the same circles."

"You haven't heard?" Corrine asked. "She has class with her. She supposedly held a door for her and got put out of Carmichael's class!"

"You're kidding, right?" Regina eyed me. "Why didn't you tell me you had class with her?" Her nostrils flared. I could see the blood rising in her face.

"I didn't even know who she was until today."

"Are you from this planet? What do you mean you *didn't know* who she was?" Regina cocked her head to the side. Clearly, I was no longer speaking English.

I shrugged. "It doesn't matter to me."

She scoffed, mumbling something inaudible under her breath. She pierced her spinach angrily.

"What did the spinach do to you?" Brandon joked, trying to lighten the situation. He looked to Corrine for backup, but she kept her head down, shoveling potatoes into her mouth.

I could tell that Regina was imagining the spinach as my eyes so I excused myself from the table, so she could vent without my presence. "I'm going to get some food."

I made my way across the cafeteria, scooting around clumps of people socializing with each other. A group of girls made eye contact with me and waved. I looked over my shoulder for Regina or Andrea, but they weren't there. Those girls were waving at *me*? I hesitantly waved back and a small feeling of satisfaction seeped through my body. Was I becoming...popular? I straightened my back. *Legacies shouldn't slouch*, I thought.

I reached for a tray at the same time someone else did.

"Oh, go ahead." I let the girl take it. She smiled over her shoulder at me. Kamilah. She must have recognized me too because she did a huge double take. Her glossy hair whipped back and forth over her shoulder. I couldn't tell if it was hers or extensions. A couple strands stuck to her shimmery pink lip shine.

"Jones, right?" Kamilah squinted.

"Yeah," I answered. She extended her hand and I shook it welcomingly. It felt like my hand could wrap twice around her small fingers.

"Listen," she started, picking up the spoon buried in the tray of mashed potatoes. She lobbed a few steaming scoops on her plate without thinking twice. She was my kind of girl already.

"Thanks for today. Carmichael can be such a hard ass. If I was late to one more class I knew he'd flunk me."

She was small in stature but her facial features were so profound. Her large brown eyes screamed innocence. Her smile was big and genuine. I liked this girl already. No wonder why Regina was so obsessed with her.

"It's no problem," I assured her. "You were right around the corner. I wasn't going to close the door on you."

"You're ballsy." She smirked. "You're the first person to stand up to Carmichael like that."

"There's no way I would let a man who wears skimpy Speedos boss me around." I would never be intimidated by a man as overcompensating as Carmichael.

"Carmichael wears *Speedos?*" Kamilah clasped her hand over her mouth in disbelief. I didn't think her eyes could get any wider.

"I work at the gym," I admitted. "So I saw him once in his suit."

"Oh, that's gold. Comedic gold." She laughed. Her personality was magnetic. From just the slightest interaction, I wanted to be around her all the time. I trailed behind her once we were out of the food line. She grabbed a fork from the silverware tray and I did the same.

"Well," she started, "See you in class…?"

"Raevyn," I supplied. "Raevyn Elizabeth Jones."

"Kamilah Renee Parker. See you around."

It was a full house back at the table and everyone's eyes were on me.

"Thought you didn't know her," Regina accused, stabbing at her spinach again.

I ignored her statement and took my usual seat beside Jeffrey. He slid his hand up my leg. He stopped right at the seat of my jeans and almost knocked the tray off the table. He let his hand linger there for a while, caressing the place where my thighs met.

My eyes met his and he read the apprehension in my face. He removed his hand promptly giving me a quizzical look. We weren't ready for that yet, but that didn't stop me from thinking about it over and over again.

I woke up a few days later to Regina's ear-splitting screams. I ripped the covers off my bed and hustled through the living room toward her room. I tripped over random pairs of shoes that were left lying around and stubbed my toe on the floor lamp. The sun was just beginning to filter through the blinds. It had to be maybe five or six in the morning. Whatever time it was, it was way too damn early to be screaming if someone wasn't dead.

"What's going on, Reggie?" I pounded on her door. "Are you okay?"

She flung the door open and it slammed against the opposite wall. "I got an invite! Me! I got an invite! All that hard work finally paid off." She pulled me in for a long hug and I thought she'd surely break my ribs in half.

"Congratulations?" I responded. "But what is it an invitation to?"

She pushed me away. "I *really* think you're from a different planet. Spring is sorority season." She flipped a small cream card out to me. A black ribbon was tied neatly at the corner. "I was picked for the preliminary selection ceremony!"

"Oh, for the one Kamilah is in?" I asked.

"Of course!" Regina squealed. "This is it, Raevyn. This is my shot."

"I hope you make it." I yawned, truly excited for Regina, no matter how my voice sounded. It was just too early in the damn morning. "I'm going back to bed." At least I thought I was, but Regina stayed up for the rest of that morning screaming with excitement at the top of her lungs.

Throughout the rest of the day Regina wasted no time telling everyone that would listen that she got pre-selected for the sorority.

"Is she supposed to tell everyone?" I whispered to Corrine while Regina was talking to a group of guys. She whipped out her card and they seemed unfazed by it all. Regina, however, didn't seem to notice that no one was as excited as she was.

"No." Corrine lowered her voice below a whisper. "She's wanted this for so long, though." Corrine explained to me all of Regina's attempts to be selected. She tried to get noticed her first semester at Fitz because of her legacy but none of the girls were impressed. Regina had to work to be chosen like everyone else. She maintained a low profile over the last year, changed her wardrobe, friends, attitude, and she finally got noticed.

"You guys weren't always friends?" I chomped down on a spoonful of Cap'n Crunch.

Corrine shook her head. "I was a loner my freshman year. I worked, went to class, and went to my room. Then I met Andrea in my Poly Sci class and she introduced me to Reggie and Brooke. But, she left before you came."

"I keep hearing about her. What happened?"

She shook her head, tossing my question away. "I'm happy Regina finally got chosen even though this is just pre-selection."

"Pre-selection?" I echoed.

"Pre-selection only lasts for one day, so if someone doesn't get an invitation, they'll have to wait until next year. Anyway, they pick a bunch of girls they like, but as the week progresses they weed out the ones that *really* want to be a Xi."

"Do you want to be one?"

"I haven't given it much thought." Corrine shrugged. "At least not like Regina. No one in my family has pledged a sorority. My dad calls them distractions, says I need to focus on school. Still, it seems cool. If I had to choose between the sororities here, the Xi's would be the one I choose."

"There are others?"

"Plenty." She laughed. "The Xi's are the ones that matter though. You really don't know anything about Fitz, huh?" She brought her spoon to her lips, sipping a steaming cup of tea.

I blushed.

"It's okay, I was the same way my freshman year," Corrine said, pushing the tea bag around with her finger.

"How'd you learn?"

"Hanging out with them." She nodded towards Regina. I spotted Andrea strutting into the cafeteria. Dark shades guarded her eyes as usual. It seemed like the wind was always in her hair when she walked. Andrea always served. "They taught me everything. I owe them a lot."

"That's sweet to say." I gulped down another spoonful of cereal when Andrea wiggled her fingers in our direction. Corrine and I returned the gesture.

"It's the truth," Corrine admitted. "If it weren't for those two I'd still be a little bookworm, hiding on the quiet floor of the library. That's why when Reggie or Drea ask me to keep something quiet, I do. That's just what friends do."

"Of course," I commented, wondering where Corrine was going with this. She was starting to ramble and I hoped she would tell me what I wanted to hear. "You're a great friend."

"I try to be. That's why I always offer to pay for limos and champagne for Andrea. I know she can't afford it anymore. It's why I enter my name in place of Regina's for her competitions." Her eyes glazed and I realized Corrine's mind was elsewhere now, like she was talking to herself, not even acknowledging what she was saying. Her voice was low. Mean. Different. Corrine buys everything for Andrea? Did she fund her whole lifestyle, too?

At that moment Andrea plopped down at the table with a huge smile on her face. "Take a look at this." She flipped the latest issue of some sleazy tabloid around to us.

"Remember that photographer on the island in Turks and Caicos?"

Corrine snapped back to reality; her bright, happy self returned in an instant. "Yeah, French guy, right?"

Andrea scoffed. "He was Italian. Honestly, Corrine, can you remember anything?"

Her cheeks flushed and I cut in. "Well, what about the guy?"

"Right." Andrea flipped a couple pages in the magazine. "Check out ya girl!" She turned it around to us and we spotted Andrea in all her bronze, naked glory smack-dab in the middle of a tabloid. She made a phony attempt at covering her goodies that were playing a severe game of peek-a-boo in the picture.

"Any press is good press." Corrine tried to sound positive for Andrea who was clearly impressed with her less than respectable appearance.

"Exactly." Andrea nodded. "What do you think?" Her eyes locked on to mine.

I flipped my wrist over, pretending to be late for something. "Gotta go."

When I arrived at Professor Carmichael's class I expected him to throw a fit. I was expecting him to not let me in, but he didn't. He didn't even look my way when I took my regular seat in the front row.

Kamilah ran in, with about thirty seconds to spare. She zoomed past my desk so quickly, all of my books crashed to the ground, sending papers scattering everywhere.

"I'm such a klutz." She laughed, joining me in gathering my papers. She handed me everything off the floor in one big pile and scampered away. "Sorry about that."

"It's okay," I responded, sorting through the papers. I shuffled through homework assignments and graded papers until I came across a small piece of cardstock with a black ribbon tied around the edge, just like the one Regina showed me that morning.

I stole a glance over my shoulder at Kamilah and she winked discreetly.

Kamilah selected me to be a Xi.

⸻

Jeffrey was the only one I could trust with telling about being selected. Between our obligations we didn't have much quality time to spend with each other. He was so consumed in studying that he barely had any time for fun. I was growing tired of seeing him exhausted and unkempt so I left a note for him through Brandon and hoped he'd understand my directions.

The itchy vest stuck to me while I waited for Jeffrey. The attendant looked down at me and back at the clock on the wall for the hundredth time. He bent down and smacked a wad of gum.

"You sure he's coming?" He pushed up his shaggy hair wiped sweat on the back of his hand. He looked over his shoulder at the empty waiting area. It'd been over thirty minutes and still there was no Jeffrey. I was starting to think he wouldn't show.

"He should be here any minute." I tugged on the vest. "Just give us a few more minutes."

"Sure thing." He flipped his hair backwards, and jumped down off the platform. His pasty knees stuck through the holes in his jeans. I unsnapped the seatbelt peeled my skin off the leather seat. I kicked the front door open. Sweat trickled down my back. Who knew when Jeffrey would show up? If I waited any longer I was going to melt off my makeup and my edges would start to curl up. I pulled off my helmet just when I spotted him at the service counter. The woman nodded in my direction and slid a set of protective gear towards him, looking him up and down. I specifically instructed him to wear jeans. I should have known casual to Jeffrey still meant wearing a bow tie and hard bottomed shoes. He stuck out like a giraffe at a petting zoo.

Jeffrey swaggered over, his lips turning slowly into a knowing smile. "Raevyn Jones." He dropped his equipment onto the hood of his waiting vehicle and I watched his cheeks flush. I felt my heart dance a bit.

"How did you do all this?" He unbuttoned his cardigan and slid his vest on. "Where the hell are we?" Jeffrey took a long look at the attendant's bleach stained KISS T-shirt and unwashed hair as he approached.

"Welcome to the race." I smiled.

He cupped his helmet under his arm. "I just can't believe you went through all this trouble for me." He rested one foot on his racecar.

"I'd do anything for you," I said matter-of-factly. Jeffrey stared at me with a mix of emotions. I couldn't tell what he was feeling. He was just staring with that goofy half-smile of his.

"Ready when you are," the attendant cut in and climbed the stairs to turn the overhead light from red to green.

I pushed the helmet back on my head and Jeffrey did the same. Before he hopped inside, he jetted over, placing his helmet to mine. Even through the gear I could feel Jeffrey's heart beating triple time for me.

January quickly melted into February and tonight was the pre-selection ceremony. I spent every waking moment tucked between the shelves of Shakespeare and Fitz history. Between my course load and learning about Xi Nu Lambda, I had little time for socializing. All I had time for was studying.

Sometimes, Jeffrey joined me in the library, but that ended quickly because we didn't do much studying, if you catch my drift.

He vowed to maintain my cover that Carmichael planned to fail me and was tacking on more work than usual. Everyone seemed to believe that quickly. Jeffrey, however, became more and more annoyed that the time we both blocked out of our schedules for each other became my extra studying time.

We met in our usual spot that night on the quiet floor near a very secluded section of the library. Sometimes, on our good nights, it felt like Jeffrey and I were the only ones in the world. Tonight was one of those nights.

When I rounded the corner, Jeffrey stood amongst a bed of rose petals and scattered flickering tea candles. A nervous laugh sputtered out before I could catch it. His face broke into a ridiculous smile too.

"Come on, I'm trying to be romantic here," he whispered, pointing to the rose petals.

"Are those real? Can you have candles in here?"

"No," he said, crestfallen. He flipped a small switch on the bottom and the light died out. "Battery operated."

He pulled me to the floor and we sat cross-legged in a circle of faux candlelight. I had to admit, it would have been pretty romantic if dusty paperbacks weren't surrounding us. But, I appreciated his efforts.

"Well." He pulled a basket from behind him. "I know initiation starts tonight and I wanted to tell you how proud I am of you. You came into Fitz with practically nothing and now you're about to be a Xi."

"Not yet." I sighed, fishing into my bag. "I still have to get through tonight and who knows what else." I pulled out my laptop. "I still have a paper to do—"

"Rae, not tonight." Jeffrey pushed my laptop away. "Can we just have this moment for us? No Xi, no honors, no exams…just us."

"You? Don't want to do work?" I scoffed. He leaned in and I tackled him, pinning his back to the ground. "How's this, then?"

"Much better." He smiled. Our bodies created a shadowy silhouette on the shelves. His warm hands tugged at my shirt. I leaned back and he pushed forward, his lips just inches from mine, when he pressed his body against mine, sending me toppling backwards.

"Say you'll be my little sorority girl," he teased, dropping his knees on my arms, pinning me to the ground. A candle stabbed my shoulder blade.

"No!" I declared, flailing helplessly under his grip.

"Don't make it harder on yourself." He laughed barely affected by my bucking legs. "All you have to do is say it and I'll let you go."

"I'm not saying it." I sputtered between laughs.

He rocked back on his knees, freeing my body. "Then say you love me."

I pushed myself up on my elbows still laughing, when I noticed his smile melted away from his face. Was he *serious*? My mind went fuzzy and the words tumbled from my mouth before I could stop them.

"I love you, Jeffrey Donnelly."

My heart could have expanded out of my chest when he said, "I love you too, Raevyn Jones."

According to the invitation we had to report to the Fitz statue at midnight. When I left the library, the campus was darker than usual. The sidewalk lights had been extinguished. I could only hear the sound of my own heartbeat and my slow breathing. Ahead, I saw the outline of the Fitz statue but no one was standing there. I checked my watch and it was midnight on the dot.

I realized I was standing in the middle of campus, in the black of night, shivering. What if this was a set-up? What if B was behind all of this? What if Kamilah was B?

As soon as that thought crossed my mind a bag dropped down over my head. A sinister laugh rang out. My heartbeat grew erratic and then something inside me snapped. I swung around and my knuckles collided with someone's jaw. Fire shot through my hands. I swung again and my fist connected again with something. Someone let out a pained *oomph* at the impact.

"Oooh, we've got a fighter."

Someone jumped on top of me and forced my arms behind my back. My wrists were zip tied. The plastic cut into my skin.

"Get yourself together!" a husky voice whispered. "Calm the fuck down, Jones."

The Xi's. Not B.

Someone pushed me. I stumbled and collided hard with the ground. I yelped, tasting grass, and a zip of pain flashed up my elbow to my shoulder. I bit the inside of my cheek to keep from crying.

"Seriously, Jones?" I recognized Kamilah's voice. She pulled me up and locked her arm in mine.

"Just walk with me, okay? Calm down before you get us caught."

"Okay," I managed to answer.

She dragged me along while I tried to picture the campus. We walked straight for a few steps and I knew we were headed towards Carmichael's building. Then we took too many quick turns, it felt like we were walking in circles for a while and then I lost track of everything. I stumbled down several steps, a door creaked open and Kamilah announced, "We're waiting on two more."

I was shoved inside. The faint glow of candlelight penetrated the bag. I collided with a girl whose knees were literally knocking against one another. What did they do to her?

We stood for what felt like an eternity when finally the door opened again and clanged closed. Several sets of footsteps pounded the floor and another body was shoved next to me. Chanel No. 5 danced around my nose.

Regina.

"We can get started," someone whispered.

"Turn around," another voice demanded. Our zip ties were cut one by one. I lost count after at least fifteen snaps of the scissors. The bag clawed at my face when it was ripped over my head. I glanced around quickly and noticed at least thirty people crammed inside the room. Someone slipped when they were spun around. The floor was saturated in straw and the walls were covered in dirt like someone carved this place out of nothing.

Regina pinched my arm. "What the hell are you doing here?" she whispered.

I shrugged, taking a look around at the other girls in the room. I noticed Andrea first towering over everyone. The shivering girl beside me was Corrine. She clutched my hand and when she noticed Regina and Andrea, her chest capsized with relief.

A tall girl with a wide nose emerged from the crowd of Xi's, clutching a plastic bag of ice to her jaw. Her eyes landed on me.

"I want this one," she declared to the group. "You're the fighter, right?"

I slinked back towards the wall. "I didn't know what was going on."

"Don't you dare speak!" Kamilah's voice shook the walls.

"You listen." She turned her attention to the group. "Your opinions are not valid here, so I advise you to keep your damn mouths closed." She paced the floor in front of us. Her eyes narrowed, giving each girl on the wall an equal once-over. She stopped right under Andrea's chin, but for a second, I thought I saw something—intimidation, maybe terror—pass over Andrea's face.

"As you *should* know I am Kamilah Renee Parker, president of Xi Nu Lambda Sorority and my sister here is Janay Michelle Young. Address us as Miss Parker or Miss Young and nothing else. Not Kamilah, not K, not Janay, we are not your fucking friends," she spat.

Janay hadn't moved from my personal space. She was still staring me down, studying every inch of my face. If I pressed my back against the wall any more I'd fall right through it.

"This is the first night of initiation. Most of you won't make it past this night," Janay stated matter-of-factly. "Especially not you." Her nose pressed against mine. "I'll make sure of that."

Kamilah explained that she was pairing us off. Our first assignment was to test our knowledge of B. W. Fitz, and I knew I was doomed. I should have studied a bit more tonight but then I remembered why I didn't study. I tried to suppress the smile that was itching to show on my face.

"There are historic landmarks all over campus." She began to hand out papers. "At these landmarks there is an object buried there. Take it."

A gasp rippled through the room and Janay smirked approvingly. "This is a combination of history and smarts. The first team to return with all the correct answers and all the artifacts will pass this round. The last team to arrive or the team with the least answers loses. Don't take it personal. Maybe you can get selected next year."

Kamilah paired Regina and I together. Regina knew almost everything about B. W. Fitz and I, well…I could run fast. I needed to make it past initiation because I wanted to wipe the smirk right off of Janay's face.

I darted out of the building and up the concrete steps with Regina by my side. Regina took me by the arm and I slowed down. A group of girls sprinted past us, dispersing across campus in their black hoods, and the night swallowed them whole.

"Come on," I begged. "They're beating us."

"Let me do this. I know this campus more than anyone." She was out of breath already.

She swallowed and added, "I know you're not a legacy." Her eyes darted between mine. "I don't know how you got in here, but I won't tell anyone, okay? Let's just do this together and get this over with."

When I didn't answer she added, "I need this, Raevyn. My whole family is in this sorority. I lost my grandmother's earrings. This will make it all right."

My heart softened at the thought of her earrings. That was my fault.

"Okay," I answered, allowing Regina to take the lead. We didn't have time to argue over facts or fiction. We could deal with that after we made it through tonight. She hugged me tight, her scent suffocating me, and I took off behind her.

With Regina's knowledge, and my all-access pass to buildings, we had the scavenger hunt in the bag. The last challenge was to take a white candle from the church. The doors were chained on the outside and while other groups were trying to determine if the question was a riddle or trick, Regina beckoned me around the building.

"There's a window," she whispered. Between her heavy breathing and our teeth chattering I had to strain my ears to understand her. "We can p-pry it open."

I nodded and she led me toward it. She pushed up on the ledge but it didn't budge. I looked around frantic for anything to help when I noticed the unchained door. The red censor blinked at me. I swiped my card and it turned green, welcoming us.

"Pssst," I whispered to Regina who had gone all Hulk on the window. Her face was turning a different color when she whipped around.

"What?" she hissed.

I threw the door open and toggled my card between my fingers. Regina and I dashed inside.

"I won't ask where you got that from," she said as we barreled down the center aisle of the sanctuary.

She made a cross over her chest. "Forgive us." I nicked the smallest candle from the candelabra and the pair of us left as easily as we came in.

We were the first back to the underground barn. Kamilah and Janay's heads knocked together when we barged in the door. Kamilah kicked the leather bound book closed and from the quick second that I laid eyes on it, it seemed like a list of names. About a dozen were scratched off. I prayed my name wasn't on there.

"Don't tell me you gave up." Janay approached me.

"We're finished," I reported. I held out the sheet to her and emptied our pockets. She turned to Kamilah who looked between the both of us.

"You're what?" She snatched Regina's paper.

"Finished," Regina echoed. "We found everything you asked for."

"That's impossible." Janay cackled. "You took a candle from the church?" I handed her the small white candle and I couldn't help but smirk when Janay said to us, "You're dismissed."

―――――――――――――――――

"Did you make it?" Regina whispered that night in the phone booth to Corrine and Andrea.

In the black of night I followed the three of them through the hallways to the booth. After the scavenger hunt, they came over and we all collapsed on the floor of the living room. Andrea stripped off her dirty Juicy Couture sweatpants.

"These are my favorite sweatpants." She threw the soiled pair in the corner of the room with our Uggs, which were now ruined too. Melted snow, mud, and other unidentified substances stuck to our clothes.

"We can go into the city tomorrow and get some more," Regina offered, kicking off her pair of ruined Uggs.

"They're my favorite." Corrine looked longingly to the corner.

"Do you really want to save those things?" I ripped off my sweatshirt and dropped into the pile. "Let's just burn it all." I laughed.

Regina's eyebrows rose. "I kind of want to keep it…at least the sweatshirt. We made it through our first Xi initiation, Rae."

All four of us met eyes and we silently celebrated our small victory. I announced to the group that I was going to bed and once I started my shower, I thought I heard the suite door snap closed. I looked out into the living room and the three of them were gone. In only a towel, I crept along the corridor, down the stairs to the phone booth where the three of them were crammed inside, whispering together.

"Yes," Andrea hissed. "Now what the hell is so important? I want to go to bed. We still have class in the morning you know."

"Quit bitching," Regina demanded. "She isn't a legacy."

The three of them were silent for a little before Corrine said, "You don't know that for sure."

"I found out today," Regina countered.

"Did she *say* she wasn't?" Corrine argued.

"You knew she wasn't," Andrea snapped. "You kept saying how weird it was that she didn't know stuff. Come on, Corrine."

"We can't keep doing this."

"Corrine, she can't come back here next year," Andrea pleaded with her. "If she comes back here she ruins everything."

Corrine begged, "She doesn't know it was us. If we just remain calm all of this will blow over. You guys are making it worse with all this sneaking around."

"Worse?" Regina shrilled. Someone promptly shushed her. "Corrine, whose side are you on here?"

"Reggie, you know I'm on your side," Corrine whined.

"We stop this now." Andrea ripped back the accordion door and I was frozen to the carpet. I willed my feet to dash quietly up the hallway when Andrea finished, "With or without your   help."

"Are you sure you even heard them correctly?" Jeffrey asked while he balanced on the top bar of the metal divider in Gary's omelette line. "It was like four in the morning." He leaned over the counter a plucked a hunk of bacon from the pan while Gary's back was turned. "You could have been imagining it."

I sucked in a huge breath of air. Jeffrey and I spent the last hour discussing what I overheard last week while Regina, Corrine and Andrea were in the phone booth. He refused to believe that they could be plotting to get me kicked out of Fitz. "Ya'll are like *besties* or whatever." He mocked Corrine's high-pitched voice.

"You're not listening to me," I hissed. The frustration in my voice was overtaken with sizzles when Gary dumped eggs into the pan. I spoke over it. "I know what I heard, Jeffrey."

"And I know Regina," Jeffrey countered, sprinkling a handful of cheese in his mouth. Gary slapped his hand away. A string of cheddar hung from his smiling lips when he said, "I really think you just need some sleep. I heard these sorority initiations are rough."

"Shhh!" I punched his shoulder.

"Ain't got to shhh him on account of me," Gary cut in. He was pretending like he wasn't listening the entire time we'd been in line. "I done seen and heard it all in these walls." He gestured his cheesy spatula around him at the green tile. "You ain't the first girl to be pledge and you won't be the last."

"See?" Jeffrey cocked his head at me. "Tell her she's overreacting, man. She's worried about nothing."

Gary shrugged. "I ain't gonna say all that now. I heard those girls do some mean things."

"Nothing mean has happened yet," I assured him, even though that was a lie. Just last night I had to console Corrine because Janay picked on her the entire night. She did a good job of keeping it together while we were in front of the Xi's, but as soon as we got home, she cried for hours asking us why they hated her.

"They hate everyone." Andrea picked cheese whiz and Cheerios out of her weave. "You ain't the only one that got it bad tonight, Corrine Rayne. Suck it up."

"Don't." Regina whipped around with eyes the size of saucers.

"I hate you," Corrine spat, stomping out of the room. I was the only one who was stunned and that was when I made up my mind to tell Jeffrey about what was going on. I thought for sure he'd at least listen to what I had to say. Instead, he was too focused on stuffing his face with his omelette fixings.

"Don't let them girls get to you." Gary pushed Jeffrey's oversized omelette across the counter, but his eyes were focused on me.

"I won't," I answered, trailing behind Jeffrey into an empty cafeteria. I grabbed two forks and we sat down at our usual table. He wasted no time digging into his food, funneling it in his mouth. He slurped down a big gulp of orange juice. I watched his jaws work, noticing the stubble that grew on his cheeks. He didn't have on a bow tie, either. I was just about to ask him what was going on when he spoke first.

"Gary's right." He covered his mouth. "You're so worried about Corrine and Andrea—"

"Your Jill too," I reminded him.

He rolled his eyes. "You just need to relax, Rae. Nobody is out to get you."

"You didn't hear them, Jeffrey! This isn't the first time they had these secret meetings about me. What if it was Regina that night outside of Dr. Rudd's office? What if they know...?" I leaned in and my lips grazed his ear. He flinched and a smile tugged at his lips. That wasn't what I was going for, but I couldn't help but to smile when I was that close to him. "What if they know about the grades?"

He sat up so fast that the back of his head almost slammed into my nose. "No one knows about that, Rae. You haven't heard from Miss Tanner, right? Or Dr. Rudd?"

"Nothing." My hands surrendered. "I swear."

He shook his head, cutting into the other half of the omelette, pushing the plate towards me. I heeded his silent request, and started to eat. "You're overreacting. Just get through this semester. Let's get you these letters so we can put this behind us."

"You realize that you just pluralized us, right?"

His eyes danced between mine.

"You know what I mean."

"You love me," I teased, pinching at his chest.

"You know." He shrugged. "You all right for a Southern girl," he said nonchalantly.

"Whatever," I laughed. He left a wet kiss on my cheek and we went back to eating. I wanted to believe that everything would be okay, but I couldn't let it go. Regina and Corrine meant business that night. They were planning something. But, what? And why against me? What did I do?

"You really think it's nothing?" I asked again when I decided enough time had passed. His shoulders slumped.

"Yes, Rae!" He slapped his hands on his thighs. "You're thinking way too deep into this. They probably weren't even talking about you. I know Regina can do some shady shit, but she wouldn't be plotting with Andrea and Corrine of all people to get you kicked out of school. What could the two of them possibly do?"

I shrugged. "It's not like they can access your grades." He pointed to himself. "They can't make anyone fail you. Hell, Carmichael already tried to fail you and he couldn't even do that."

I shrugged again.

"But what about Brooke Wheeler?"

"Who?"

"The girl I replaced. She was Regina's roommate, wasn't she?"

"She had a death in the family," Jeffrey said. "Her grandmother, I think. Her mother went crazy. She had to be put in a crazy house, and then Brooke left, too. Her whole life was falling apart, Rae. Nothing but a coincidence that she was Regina's roommate."

I fiddled with my fingers.

Jeffrey's hand landed on my thigh. He tugged at the stitching on my jeans. "Come 'ere."

I straddled him, wrapping my arms around his neck.

"Put this out of your head, Raevyn Jones," he demanded. His mouth was so close to mine. Fire pranced between our bodies. His hands massaged the small of my back. A soft moan tumbled out of my lips and he pulled me closer until I couldn't tell where his skin ended and mine began. I buried my face in his neck. Stubble scratched my cheek, snapping me out of his trance.

"You need to cut that." I hopped up, pulled my backpack on my shoulder and took our dirty dishes to the trash.

He scurried behind me. "And you need to give me some of that." He swatted at my butt.

"In your dreams, Jeffrey," I sang, blowing him an air kiss.

***

The days began to run together. Between the initiation into Xi Nu Lambda that had me up at all hours of the night, coupled with my course load and my work schedule, I was losing track of time. There weren't enough hours in the day. Midterms were upon us and just like at finals time last semester, people moved like zombies.

Work. School, Xi was all I thought about. Despite what Jeffrey said, I kept feeling that I had to tread lightly around Regina, Andrea, and Corrine. They always acted normal, but I knew they were plotting something. I knew the best way to get revenge was to ensure that I would be enrolled in B. W. Fitz next semester with Xi Nu Lambda letters on my chest.

I kept my head down and bolted across campus towards the library. Jeffrey had already been there since it opened. The pressure of not passing midterms and not securing an honors blazer next year was starting to eat away at him.

I reached the quiet floor of the library and was seconds away from pushing the door open when I noticed him digging in his bag for something. He found a small prescription bottle and poured a few white pills into the palm of his hands. He tossed them in his mouth and swallowed. He buried the bottle back in the bottom of his bag and glanced around to see whom, if anyone, had been watching and that's when he and I met eyes.

His eyes were tired. His face lined with exhaustion and excess facial hair like he hadn't showered in days. He didn't look like *my* Jeffrey. A nauseating feeling stirred inside. How did I miss the signs again?

"Hey," he said, turning back around to his work. Dozens of books were open the desk. Scribbled notes trailed along the edges with arrows that pointed to large highlighted chunks of text.

"What was that?" I asked.

"This? W-World History. My exam is tomorrow and I need an A." His hands trembled when he turned the page.

"That's not what I'm talking about." I slammed my books down beside him. "What the hell did you just take?" Before I could reach for his chin, he pulled away.

"Worry about you, Raevyn," he ordered. "I'm fine."

"Is that what you were taking during finals last semester? What is that?"

When he didn't answer I lunged for his bag. He ripped it back and the leather handle popped from the side. His bag flipped upside down, sending the contents flying all over the room. Bottles of pills clattered to the ground, uncapping, and launched multi-colored pills all over the carpet. Some rolled to a stop or disappeared under a bookcase. He dove on the floor after them but it was too late. I had seen enough.

"When's the last time you've slept?" I watched him while he feverishly packed his bag. He threw the stray pills into any of the open bottles and secured the lids. The bottles hit the bottom of his bag with a rattle—the same rattle I *knew* I heard last year the day he asked me to the Mason ball.

"I don't know," he admitted. "A couple days ago? Listen, I need to pass these classes. I need this blazer next year."

I couldn't think of any words to say. I was too disappointed to yell and my heart was hammering too loudly in my chest to hear his excuses. I knew how much his legacy meant but he was killing himself over something he didn't even *want* to do.

"Can you keep this between us?"

"If you stop taking them." I crossed my arms over my chest. "Today."

"Raevyn." He drew my name out like a child who couldn't have a cupcake before dinner. "I can't just stop. I need this."

"You can!" He sounded like my mother—weak and pathetic. "You think you can take one pill to stay awake to finish just one assignment and then it turns into two pills to stay level-headed." I quoted my mom. His eyes softened. "Then it turns into taking one every day until you don't even know what it feels like to be sober. By that time, it's a full blown addiction."

"I'm not—"

"You're not addicted, huh?" I scowled. "You sound just like her." I flung my bag over my shoulder. "I don't want any part of this. If you want to kill yourself over some stupid blazer, you go right ahead. I don't want to see it."

"It's not just some stupid blazer," he roared. The chair toppled over. "I wish you would stop saying that."

"Excuse me, it's honors," I contested, tossing air quotes around the word. "Because that's *so* worth dying for."

"You wouldn't understand. I have to work for my GPA. Nobody magically changes mine."

Blood sprinted through my veins. "Don't you dare," I warned. My hand curled into a ball before I could stop it.

"I'm sorry," he backtracked. "Raevyn, listen to me. I'm sorry."

"I have to do this. You know my legacy. My mother's a doctor. My father is a lawyer. Both of my parents graduated from Fitz at the top of their class. I'm just Jeffrey." His eyes welled with tears and he cradled his head in his arms. "Everyone is counting on me, Rae, I have to do this. This is the only thing that helps."

"You don't have to do anything." My heart broke in two. I knelt beside him. I spoke softly, "Jeffrey, listen to me. You don't have to do this to yourself. Your parents will love you regardless if you're Jeffrey the lawyer or Jeffrey my race car driver."

More tears spilled down his cheeks, and I hurried to wipe them away. He had the power to choose. He didn't have to do what his parents did. He could be whomever he wanted. We could do whatever we wanted.

"I can't be a failure." His words tumbled out amidst the onslaught of sobs, and I wondered how many nights everyone around here spent crying about their own legacies.

"There is not a failing bone in your body." I pinched at his chest. "You're more than enough, babe." His lips trembled, but after a little more tickling, he finally smiled.

He pulled me off the ground and I fell into the curves of his body. His arms wrapped tightly around my small frame and I remembered all the times my mother promised me she'd quit. I flashbacked to the dozens of times she and I cried together and flushed her pills down the toilet. That was before she overdosed last Christmas. I wouldn't know what I would do if I lost Jeffrey to the same demon.

"I'll quit," he said, kissing me gently on the chin. I brought my face down to his and swung my legs over his lap.

"You promise me, Jeffrey."

"Raevyn Elizabeth Jones, I promise you."

We locked pinkies and I lost track of time when his lips touched mine.

⸻

At dinner one night, Regina and I received the same text message from Kamilah: **Tonight at midnight. Fitz Statue.**

Shortly after, I heard Corrine's phone ring and then like dominoes, so did Andrea's.

"Tell me this is going to end soon." Andrea flopped back on the couch. "I'm starting to wish I hadn't listened to you." She shot Regina an annoyed look. "You said this would be fun. Look at the bags under my eyes! I've been missing photo ops because I sleep through the photo shoots!"

"It should be over any day now," Corrine said. There had been many days we had to convince Corrine to stay strong during the initiations. She wanted to quit at least once a week.

"Corrine's right," Regina added. Her hair, messy and tangled, was brought up into a bun. I'd never seen her go so long without make-up. "Mom says it should be ending soon." She threw her phone on the table alongside Andrea and Corrine's and stretched.

I struggled to pull myself off the couch. My limbs were heavy with fatigue. "Let's just get tonight over with." I yawned.

We all threw on our black hoodies and dispersed in different directions once we left the dormitory. As the fastest, I arrived at the Fitz statue first and waited for the bag to be placed over my head. It got easier each time it occurred; at least I didn't slug anyone. I was sure Janay was thankful for that.

While I was being led down the narrow steps towards the underground barn I felt my pocket vibrate. I silenced my phone, berating myself for forgetting to leave it in my room. I fell in line beside Corrine hoping that whomever it was would get the hint and not call back. Then, it rang again almost immediately.

"Is that your phone?" Corrine asked through her bag.

"I forgot to leave it," I answered. I dug my hand in my pocket and silenced it again. I fumbled in my pocket searching for the button to turn it off. I swiped blindly at the screen.

"What are you doing, Jones?" Kamilah barked. I dropped my hand by my side. I felt it vibrate over and over again almost nonstop. Who could be calling me at this time of the night? It could have been Wade or Antoine calling to threaten me again. Or worse, B. My father crossed my mind and I said a quick prayer that my mother was okay.

The room filled up with bodies and our hoods were ripped off, bringing me back to the present moment.

Kamilah, Janay, and the slew of other Xi's were cloaked head to toe in white, like angels. Their long skirts swept the floor angelically. The edges of the fabric were starting to brown in the moments where it rested on the dirty floor. Each woman held a candle. I counted ten, one of each of the initiates. Corrine slapped my hand discreetly.

Tonight was the night I was becoming a Xi.

My eyes met Regina's across the room and tears formed in the corners of her eyes. I was happier for her than any of us. This is what she wanted more than anything. Corrine, Andrea, and I just so happened to get chosen. Regina actually worked for it.

"Welcome, initiates, to the sisterhood of Xi Nu Lambda." Kamilah smiled. The candlelight waved across her cheeks making them appear larger, almost cartoon-like. "Tonight, you will no longer be addressed as an initiate—"

"Or bitch," someone chimed in. A pathetic ripple of laughter echoed around the room.

"You all are my sisters," Kamilah continued.

Janay walked over to each of us, placing a candle in our hands and lighting it.

"Let this, my sisters, be a symbol of the magnetic light we carry across this campus and essentially the world. Ladies, you all are now officially apart of the sisterhood of Xi Nu Lambda Sorority."

My phone vibrated again and the sound seemed to amplify in our cramped quarters. We were specifically instructed to leave our phones at home every single night and the one night I forget, is the night I get initiated.

Great.

Everyone began to look around besides Corrine and me. We knew where the sound was coming from. I held my breath until Janay approached me.

"Go ahead. Answer it," she instructed. "We're not busy at all."

I dug in my pocket and saw Brandon's number on the caller ID.

"I'm so sorry, Miss Young," I pleaded. "I don't know why he's calling me."

"It's a *he*!" she announced to the group who snickered in response. "Booty call?"

I turned around and I felt everyone's eyes glued to my back.

"What *is* it?" I snapped.

"Thank God you answered!" Brandon howled. Sirens wailed in the background.

"It's Jeffrey. I tried everyone, no one was answering. I – I didn't know what to do," he sputtered.

I dug one finger in my ear. "What about him?"

"I walked in..." I could barely understand him from the sirens and the sobbing. "...I walked in and he w-wasn't breathing!"

I gripped the wall to keep me from falling. A million thoughts flashed simultaneously through my mind. I steeled myself. "Where are you?"

"You have to c-come, Raevyn! He wasn't br-breathing. I can't do this al-lone."

I felt someone's hand on my back willing me to turn around. I clutched the phone until my fingers pained.

"What's going on?" Corrine's face looked distorted through my tears.

I didn't know what to say. How could I leave right now? Regina's eyes locked onto mine and I turned around to Kamilah, whose face darkened with disappointment.

"I gotta go," I said.

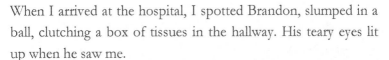

When I arrived at the hospital, I spotted Brandon, slumped in a ball, clutching a box of tissues in the hallway. His teary eyes lit up when he saw me.

"Raevyn." He reached out for me, pulling me in close. "No one else was answering. I called all of you. Where is Regina?" He looked over my shoulder for her. Of course he expected her, the Jill. He looked my muddy uniform up and down. I had no time to change.

"What are you wearing?"

"Where is he? Which room?"

Brandon's shaky finger pointed to the room just ahead where the door was cracked. I rushed over and saw my Jeffrey. Wires protruded out of his body. A machine expelled steady beeps next to him. His eyes were closed, but he still looked exhausted.

"Jeffrey," I whispered, battling between wanting to scream at him or climb in bed with him. "Why'd you do this to me?" I wanted to punch him and I wanted to hold him all at the same time.

"I'm sorry." A pudgy nurse appeared in the door. "You really can't be in here." She glanced back over her shoulder, down at her chart, and then swiped at her wide pig nose. "You gotta go, okay?"

"This is my boyfriend," I managed to squeak out. "I just got here. Please, just give me a few minutes."

She shifted her weight. "By the time I finish this floor, I expect you to be gone, okay? You got about ten minutes." I thanked her and she closed the door behind herself.

I climbed in bed beside Jeffrey, like I had with my mom several times before, and clutched his hand, planting soft kisses on his cheek.

"I'm here," I whispered to his sleeping body. I knew his mind was miles away from here. "I'll never leave you." I linked his lifeless fingers in mine and after I said a few silent prayers sleep finally took me.

The sun peeked through the blinds jolting me awake. I cracked my eyes open, shielding them from the harassing light. My back ached when I stretched. My body felt like I'd been in a fight. I thought my mind was playing tricks on me when I reached over to find an empty bed.

No wires.

No beeping machine.

No Jeffrey.

I bolted up in bed, a scream lodged in my throat, when my fingers brushed a slip of paper.

If you tell anyone, you'll be dead next. I told you to get out a long time ago. – B.

Read on for an excerpt from the next book in
The Birthright Trilogy

THE MISSING

Coming in 2014

Detective Douglas hadn't returned to the interrogation room in what felt like hours. The ticking clock reminded me ever so often how long I'd been here, cold and alone. I pulled my ratty Xi initiation hoodie that was covered in weeks of old sweat around me. The tear-soaked sleeves clung to my bare wrists. I fidgeted in the steel chair and caught a full, horrifying view of myself in the two-way mirror across the room.

My eyes were almost swollen shut from all the crying I'd done. My hair was dry and filthy, sticking out all over the place like a lunatic's. And maybe I was going crazy because I had no idea how I ended up here again.

Everything was going so smoothly, and with one phone call it all fell apart. I fingered a note and Regina's Chanel earrings hidden deep in the pocket of my hoodie. A chill slithered down my back every time I thought about last night. One minute I was with Jeffrey, holding his limp hand, and listening to his steady heartbeat and the next minute he was gone.

Was he dead? Did he leave? And why was I here? What did *I* do?

I buried the heel of my palm into my forehead. Why couldn't I remember? The soft taps of shoes echoed outside the door. Detective Douglas swung the door open and loped inside.

His face was lined either with irritation or exhaustion, I couldn't tell. He clutched a manila file under his arm and a Styrofoam cup of coffee.

The tight-lipped man took a seat across from me and ran long fingers through his shaggy, dark hair. He took a look over his shoulder at the two-way mirror. My eyes followed his, but all I could see were the two of us. I knew someone was behind there, watching.

He slid the cup of coffee towards me and, as much as I wanted to take it, I refused. My body was still groggy from sleep deprivation over the last few months of Xi initiation. No wonder I didn't wake up when Jeffrey left the bed. My stomach flipped inside out. Where was he?

"Take this," he offered. "You need it more than me."

"I'm alright," I squeaked. My throat stung. "I just want to go home."

The detective's tired eyes sprang to life. He flipped his file open and my mug shot slid across the table toward me. I didn't even recognize myself in the picture even though it was hardly a year ago. My hair looked like someone turned me upside down and mopped their floor. My cheeks were sunken and my face was drained of color. My collarbone jutted out of my skin, evidence that I'd been missing too many meals. My fingernails were chomped down to the cuticles. I remembered being terrified that day, just as I was now. Somehow, even though I was miles away from Antoine, I landed myself in a police station again.

"And where exactly is home, Raevyn?" He reached over and pulled the abandoned coffee cup towards him and took a long sip. He eyed me over the rim.

The room suddenly grew cold like all the heat had been sucked out of the world. I pulled my arms into my sweatshirt. I hoped no one from my school was on the other side of that mirror. I looked up apprehensively but I could only see my solemn reflection and the back of the detective's head. Still, I couldn't risk saying anything about my old life in Maryland.

"What do you want from me?" I begged. "What am I even doing here?"

He cleared his throat. "Raevyn, how long have you been a student at Fitz?"

I shrugged. A million thoughts ran through my mind. I had to be smart about what I was going to say. "I think you know the answers to all the questions you're asking me. Why am I here?" I repeated, digging deep inside myself to funnel some authority into my voice.

His mouth parted to speak, and then a slow, malicious smirk spread over his face. He shook his head and pulled another picture out of the file.

I immediately recognized the handsome boy. I drank in his familiar image. His slim face and beautiful brown eyes that were so mysteriously dark they were almost black. His perfectly groomed goatee sat beneath his wide nose and lined his unbelievably soft, full lips, which spoke the sweetest, most sincere words to me. Just looking at his dazzling smile made my heart flutter. I could still feel the way his goatee scratched against the side of my face when I cuddled next to him last night.

My Jeffrey.

He was smiling back at me. His arms were wrapped around his mother and father's shoulders. His bowtie askew, and his graduation cap sat lopsided on his head. This must have been his high school graduation. It was the only time his mother and father had been together in the same room, I remembered. His mother kissed his cheek. A large diamond, the size of a dime, adorned her ring finger. His father had one hand clutching a cell phone to his ear, and the other wrapped around his son's shoulders like he posed for the picture amidst a phone call.

Trembling, I pulled the picture towards me, running my finger along the curves of Jeffrey's smile. *Where are you?*

"Do you know him?"

Tears tumbled down my cheeks. I wiped them away quickly. "Jeffrey Vincent Eugene Donnelly the fourth," I murmured.

"And who is he to you?"

"My boyfriend." I swallowed the sob that bubbled in my throat.

"I need you to tell me what happened last night, Raevyn." Detective Douglas looked at me with accusing eyes. "Everything you can remember."

"I told you at the hospital." I croaked. "I have no idea what happened to him." I fingered the note in my pocket again. "I woke up and he was just…gone."

"Just gone?" he repeated. Sarcasm laced his words. "You can't expect me to buy that."

"All I know is that Jeffrey wasn't there when I woke up."

"What'd you do, Raevyn? You get in a fight with him? You pay Antoine to come get rid of him?"

My heart dropped out of my chest. "W-what did you say? You think *I* did this?" My voice came out soft even though I wanted to be angry. My whole body began to tremble.

Detective Douglas squared his shoulders to me. "You haven't heard? Your *real* boyfriend coincidentally makes bail the same night Jeffrey goes missing. Doesn't seem like that much of a coincidence to me at all, actually." He leaned back, his eyes searching for something between mine. I was rooted to my chair in disbelief, too much in shock to think. My blood ran cold. Erratic thoughts zipped through my mind at the same time, all reaching one destination. Could Antoine be B? Could he be the one that wrote the note? Would he do that? Would he *kill* Jeffrey?

At that moment the door to the interrogation room flew open. Warmth washed the walls of the small room. Goose bumps prickled on my skin. Detective Douglas jumped up when a stranger bounded inside. His chair scraped against the floor and slammed against the two-way mirror, our reflections rippled like a fun house mirror.

A tall, stoic man stood in the doorway, clutching a brief case. Thin glasses sat on the edge of his slim nose, shielding his curious green eyes. A sweet smelling cologne danced around him. He slammed his leather briefcase on the table.

"Young lady don't say another word."

I clammed up, heeding his advice. I discreetly slipped the picture of Jeffrey off the table and into my pocket while Detective Douglas and the man argued.

"Marvin Williams of Williams and Associates." He stuck his hand out for the detective to shake but he refused. His gold cufflinks glittered in the overhead lights. "Unless you are charging Miss Jones with something, I suggest you let my client go."

I looked back and forth between the men. The detective stared him down but didn't say a word.

"This isn't over," Detective Douglas warned. He grabbed the file off the table in a hurry.

Mr. Williams looked down at me. His eyes smiled. "Let's get you home, honey." He offered me his arm and I took it, realizing my knees had turned to putty. He clutched my side as we both journeyed through the police station. Detective Douglas stood by, conversing with a few other officers who shot me disapproving glances while we journeyed out of the station.

"I'm Corrine's father. She called me frantic a few hours ago and said her best friend was in trouble. I got on the first flight."

A ray of happiness shot through my heart. Corrine was the only person who could make me smile in a time like this. When Mr. Williams and I reached the parking lot I realized the sky had grown dark and impenetrable. I'd been at the police station all day, like I thought.

Just ahead, a sliver BMW's headlights blinked at us. "Can you stand?"

I nodded as I traveled to the passenger side and slid inside.

"We don't have to talk about it today." Mr. Williams started his engine. "From the looks of things, you need a good night's sleep and a hot meal."

My stomach gurgled at the mere mention of nourishment. But, the thought of eating while Jeffrey was gone was sickening. I rested my pounding head on the cool window. It soothed my headache just for a little while.

"You came all the way from Chicago?"

"Yes," he answered curtly. It was obvious he was not a fan of small talk. "Raevyn, I need to know everything you know about what happened last night, this morning, and anything else you can think of."

Images flashed through my mind of the night before. I was getting initiated into Xi Nu Lambda, the best sorority at my school, when I got a call saying Jeffrey was in the hospital. I stayed the night with Jeffrey, sleeping next to his unconscious body, and when I woke up he was gone.

Mr. Williams pulled up to the South gate of Benjamin Wallace Fitzgerald University. The black decorative wrought iron gates made my heart leap with joy. I was home. They opened slowly at our arrival.

I noticed Corrine Williams' small frame sprinting towards us, cloaked in white. Not far behind were my other friends, Regina Fitzgerald and Andrea Terrell. Mr. Williams quickly programmed his number into my phone.

"You get a good night's rest," he advised. "When you wake up, don't say anything to anyone. You call me. I'll pick you up and we can talk, okay?" His green eyes bore into mine.

"Yes, sir." I answered.

Corrine, Andrea, and Regina were closer now, waiting at the edge of the campus. "Don't say anything." Mr. Williams nodded in their direction. "To anyone."

I followed him out the car. Corrine ran over and flung her arms around my neck, her eyes watery.

"God, I didn't know what to do! You just left and Brandon said Jeffrey was d-dead and I—" she hiccupped, burying her face in my neck. "They wouldn't let us go. They wouldn't release us."

Regina cupped her mouth, stifling a soft sob. Her hair shrouded her face. Andrea draped her long arms around Regina's neck, resting her head on her shoulder. Corrine released me and moved on to her father.

"Thank you," she sputtered. "I didn't k-know what else to d-do, Dad."

"You did the right thing." He looked lovingly into her matching green eyes. "I want you four to go back inside and get some rest. Raevyn, you call me tomorrow."

Our heads nodded in adherence. We watched as he rounded the circle and his lights disappeared around Fitzgerald Avenue. It all felt so surreal, like something out of a movie. The four of us walked arm in arm, supporting each other, through campus toward our dorm. It was the same path I'd walked with Jeffrey just a few short months ago.

ACKNOWLEDGEMENTS

I will always thank God for granting my dreams. I prayed for it. I begged and cried for it. I worked for it and then You gave it to me. There is no one like You.

It would be a terrible tragedy not to mention my second grade teacher, Mr. Starr, who was the very first person who told me that I could be a writer. Also to Professor Lieb, who told me I would never be a writer. I thank the both of you.

Thank you to my family who has always been in support of my writing. Now you know why I've always been quiet. I've got too much stuff running around in my mind. I'll get you that tub, Mommy. I promise.

A huge thank you to Michelle Chester, the first person to read this manuscript. Thank you for putting up with me, Raevyn and B for so long. To my best friends, you have encouraged me beyond belief. I love you all more than words can say.

A double thank you goes to Todd Hunter who answered all of my annoying emails without complaint, and a triple thank you goes to Ashley West, my soul sister and publicist, who continually sees something in me that I can't seem to find within myself.

I have to thank you, the reader. Everything stems from you. Writing would not have been an option for me, if I had not been first, a reader. So, if you read the whole book or even if you read the first line and shelved it, from the bottom of my heart, I thank you.

And lastly, to the dreamer who is still afraid to take his or her own leap of faith, jump. Ignore the voices that tell you no. Concentrate on your dream. Focus on the goal.

It will be hard. There will be days where you feel like giving up, but remember; with great risk will always, always be a great reward. Take the road less traveled. Struggle now and flourish later.

In the words of the great Albus Dumbledore, "Dark and difficult times lie ahead. Soon we must all face the choice between what is right and what is easy."

xo,
Necole

P.S. - I'm always available!
Facebook: www.facebook.com/NecoleRyse
Twitter and Instagram: @necoleryse

ABOUT THE AUTHOR

Necole Ryse graduated from Towson University with a bachelor's degree in Mass Communications. Bored with life as an adult she decided to pursue a career fiction and hasn't looked back. She enjoys chocolate covered pretzels, binge watching Criminal Minds marathons, and all things Harry Potter.

47444515R10152

Made in the USA
Lexington, KY
06 December 2015